THE ADVENTURES OF THE GRAND VIZIER IZNOGOUD
BY GOSCINNY & TABARY

IZNOGOUD
AND
THE MAGIC CARPET

SCRIPT: GOSCINNY　　　　**DRAWING: TABARY**

Cardiff Libraries
www.cardiff.gov.uk/libraries

Llyfrgelloedd Caerdyd
www.caerdydd.gov.uk/llyfrgelloe

9th CINEBOOK

Many thanks to Skot Kirkwood for his support
and his website www.iznogoudworld.com.
The Publisher

Original title: Le tapis magique

Original edition: © Editions TABARY, 1991, by Goscinny & Tabary

Lettering and text layout: Imadjinn sarl
Printed in Spain by Just Colour Graphic

This edition published in Great Britain in 2010 by
Cinebook Ltd
56 Beech Avenue,
Canterbury, Kent
CT4 7TA
www.cinebook.com

A CIP catalogue record for this book
is available from the British Library

978-1-84918-044-3

9th CINEBOOK
The 9th Art Publisher

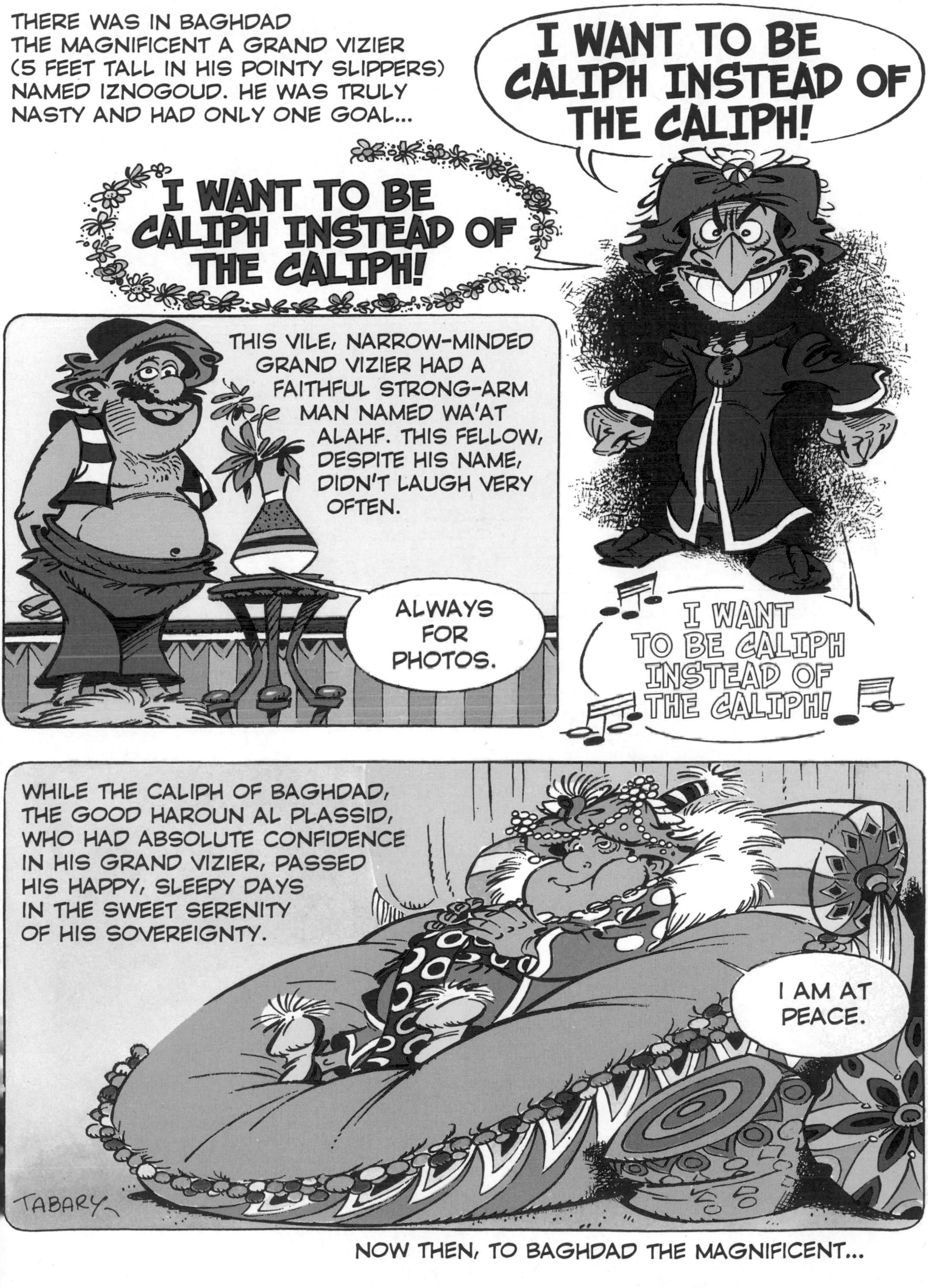
THERE WAS IN BAGHDAD THE MAGNIFICENT A GRAND VIZIER (5 FEET TALL IN HIS POINTY SLIPPERS) NAMED IZNOGOUD. HE WAS TRULY NASTY AND HAD ONLY ONE GOAL...
I WANT TO BE CALIPH INSTEAD OF THE CALIPH!
I WANT TO BE CALIPH INSTEAD OF THE CALIPH!
THIS VILE, NARROW-MINDED GRAND VIZIER HAD A FAITHFUL STRONG-ARM MAN NAMED WA'AT ALAHF. THIS FELLOW, DESPITE HIS NAME, DIDN'T LAUGH VERY OFTEN.
ALWAYS FOR PHOTOS.
I WANT TO BE CALIPH INSTEAD OF THE CALIPH!
WHILE THE CALIPH OF BAGHDAD, THE GOOD HAROUN AL PLASSID, WHO HAD ABSOLUTE CONFIDENCE IN HIS GRAND VIZIER, PASSED HIS HAPPY, SLEEPY DAYS IN THE SWEET SERENITY OF HIS SOVEREIGNTY.
I AM AT PEACE.
TABARY
NOW THEN, TO BAGHDAD THE MAGNIFICENT...

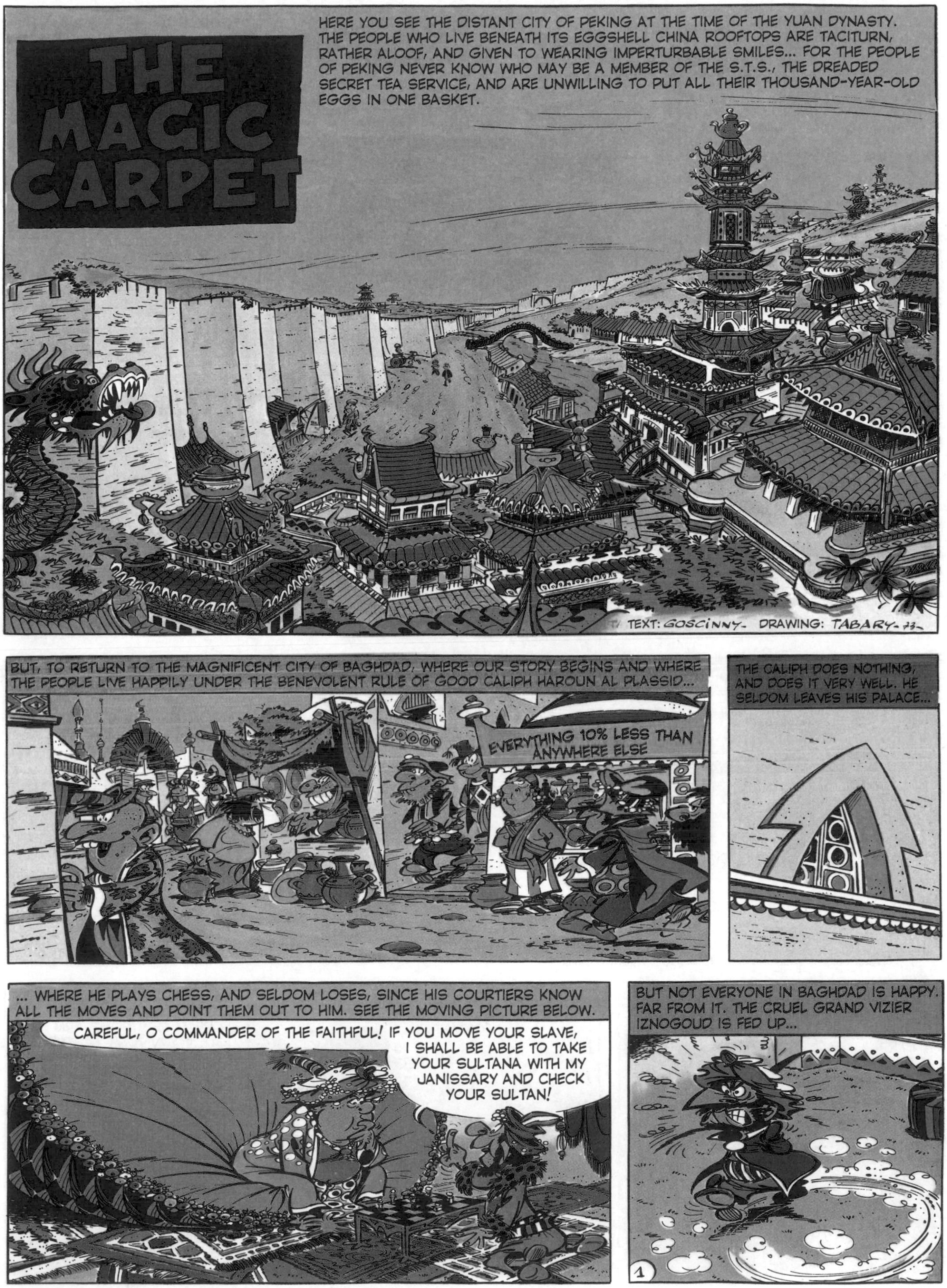
THE MAGIC CARPET
HERE YOU SEE THE DISTANT CITY OF PEKING AT THE TIME OF THE YUAN DYNASTY. THE PEOPLE WHO LIVE BENEATH ITS EGGSHELL CHINA ROOFTOPS ARE TACITURN, RATHER ALOOF, AND GIVEN TO WEARING IMPERTURBABLE SMILES... FOR THE PEOPLE OF PEKING NEVER KNOW WHO MAY BE A MEMBER OF THE S.T.S., THE DREADED SECRET TEA SERVICE, AND ARE UNWILLING TO PUT ALL THEIR THOUSAND-YEAR-OLD EGGS IN ONE BASKET.
TEXT: GOSCINNY- DRAWING: TABARY-73-
BUT, TO RETURN TO THE MAGNIFICENT CITY OF BAGHDAD, WHERE OUR STORY BEGINS AND WHERE THE PEOPLE LIVE HAPPILY UNDER THE BENEVOLENT RULE OF GOOD CALIPH HAROUN AL PLASSID...
EVERYTHING 10% LESS THAN ANYWHERE ELSE
THE CALIPH DOES NOTHING, AND DOES IT VERY WELL. HE SELDOM LEAVES HIS PALACE...
... WHERE HE PLAYS CHESS, AND SELDOM LOSES, SINCE HIS COURTIERS KNOW ALL THE MOVES AND POINT THEM OUT TO HIM. SEE THE MOVING PICTURE BELOW.
CAREFUL, O COMMANDER OF THE FAITHFUL! IF YOU MOVE YOUR SLAVE, I SHALL BE ABLE TO TAKE YOUR SULTANA WITH MY JANISSARY AND CHECK YOUR SULTAN!
BUT NOT EVERYONE IN BAGHDAD IS HAPPY. FAR FROM IT. THE CRUEL GRAND VIZIER IZNOGOUD IS FED UP...
1

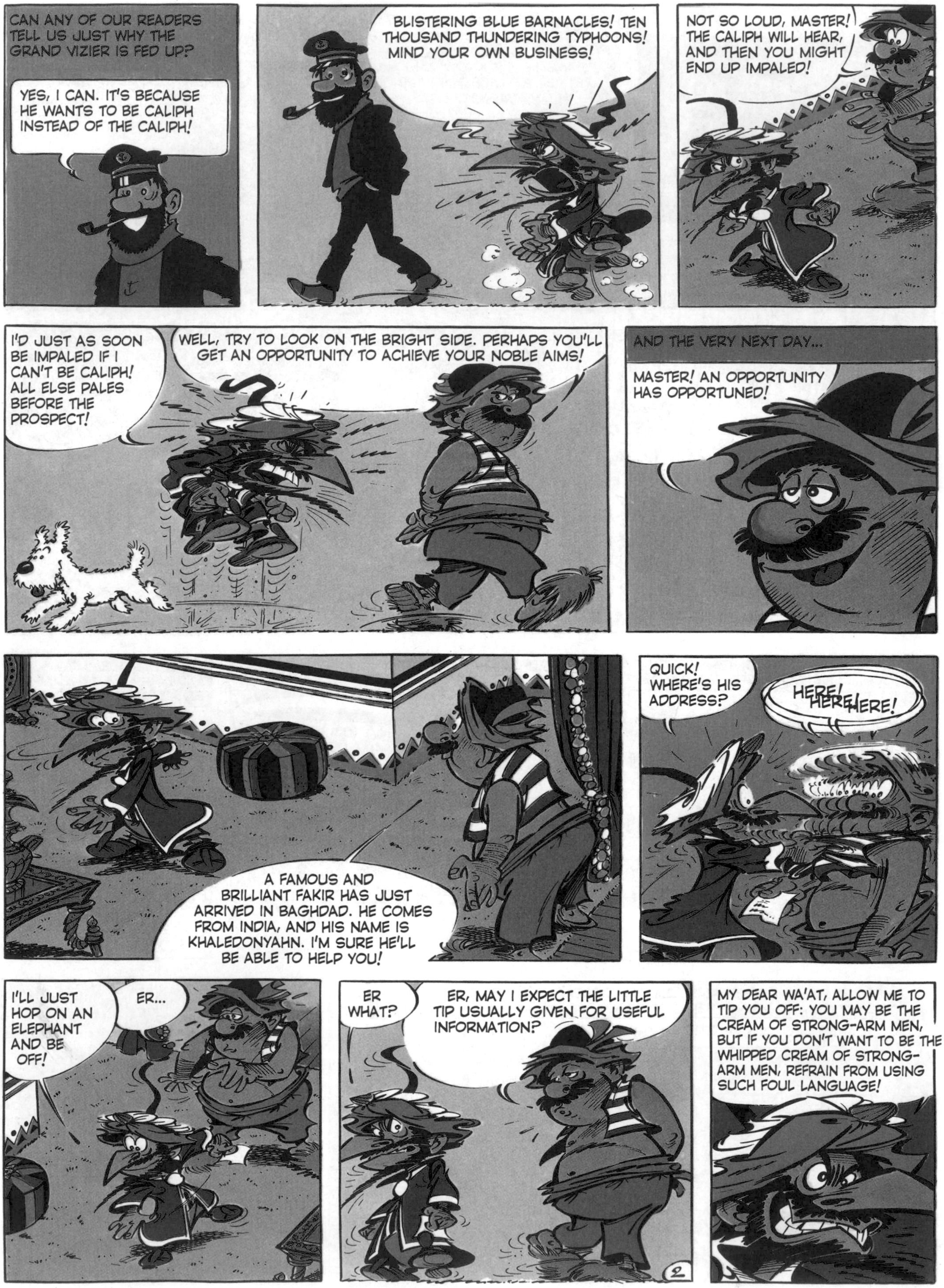
CAN ANY OF OUR READERS TELL US JUST WHY THE GRAND VIZIER IS FED UP?
YES, I CAN. IT'S BECAUSE HE WANTS TO BE CALIPH INSTEAD OF THE CALIPH!
BLISTERING BLUE BARNACLES! TEN THOUSAND THUNDERING TYPHOONS! MIND YOUR OWN BUSINESS!
NOT SO LOUD, MASTER! THE CALIPH WILL HEAR, AND THEN YOU MIGHT END UP IMPALED!
I'D JUST AS SOON BE IMPALED IF I CAN'T BE CALIPH! ALL ELSE PALES BEFORE THE PROSPECT!
WELL, TRY TO LOOK ON THE BRIGHT SIDE. PERHAPS YOU'LL GET AN OPPORTUNITY TO ACHIEVE YOUR NOBLE AIMS!
AND THE VERY NEXT DAY...
MASTER! AN OPPORTUNITY HAS OPPORTUNED!
A FAMOUS AND BRILLIANT FAKIR HAS JUST ARRIVED IN BAGHDAD. HE COMES FROM INDIA, AND HIS NAME IS KHALEDONYAHN. I'M SURE HE'LL BE ABLE TO HELP YOU!
QUICK! WHERE'S HIS ADDRESS?
HERE! HERE! HERE!
I'LL JUST HOP ON AN ELEPHANT AND BE OFF!
ER...
ER WHAT?
ER, MAY I EXPECT THE LITTLE TIP USUALLY GIVEN FOR USEFUL INFORMATION?
MY DEAR WA'AT, ALLOW ME TO TIP YOU OFF: YOU MAY BE THE CREAM OF STRONG-ARM MEN, BUT IF YOU DON'T WANT TO BE THE WHIPPED CREAM OF STRONG-ARM MEN, REFRAIN FROM USING SUCH FOUL LANGUAGE!
2

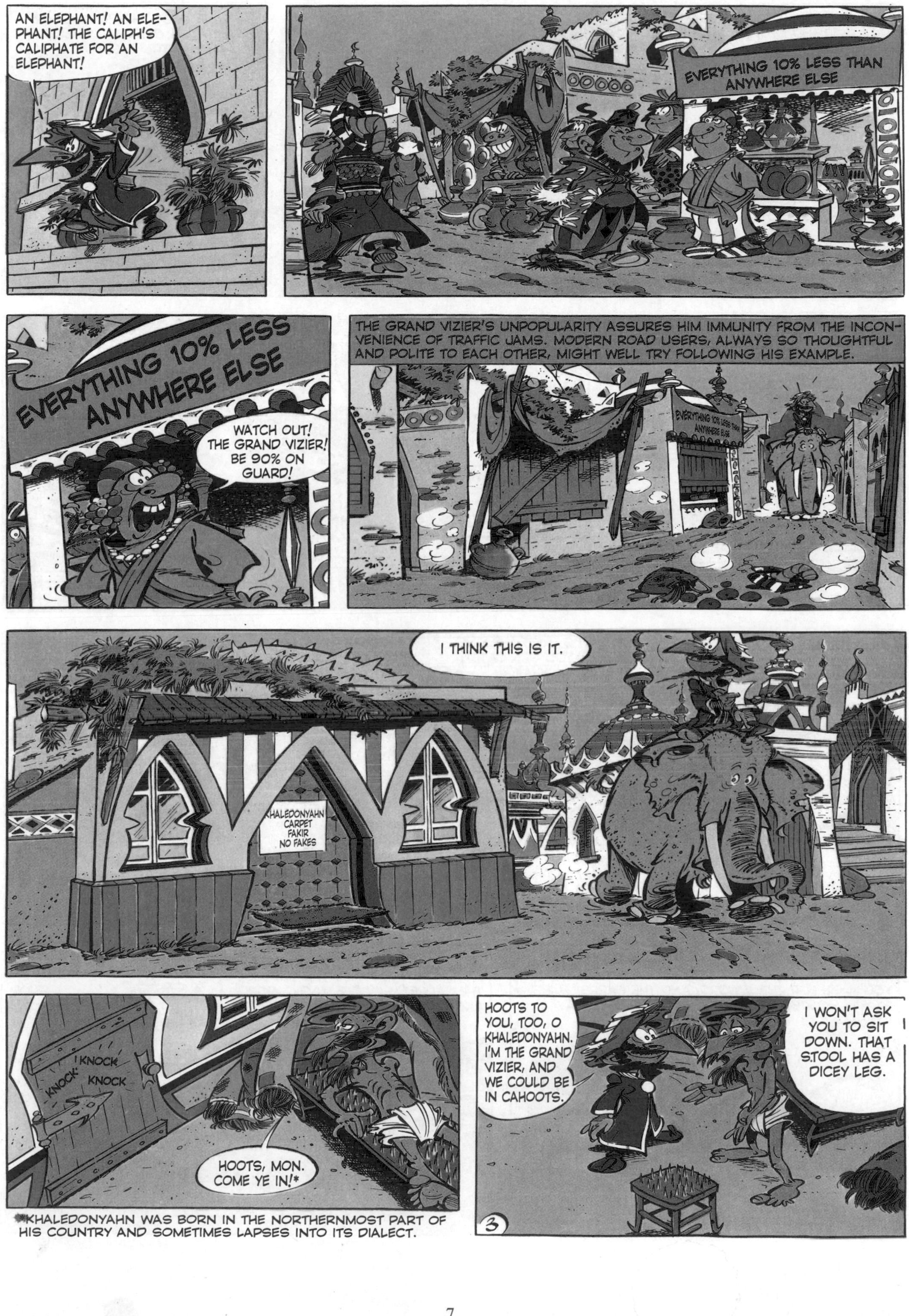
AN ELEPHANT! AN ELEPHANT! THE CALIPH'S CALIPHATE FOR AN ELEPHANT!
EVERYTHING 10% LESS THAN ANYWHERE ELSE
EVERYTHING 10% LESS ANYWHERE ELSE
WATCH OUT! THE GRAND VIZIER! BE 90% ON GUARD!
THE GRAND VIZIER'S UNPOPULARITY ASSURES HIM IMMUNITY FROM THE INCONVENIENCE OF TRAFFIC JAMS. MODERN ROAD USERS, ALWAYS SO THOUGHTFUL AND POLITE TO EACH OTHER, MIGHT WELL TRY FOLLOWING HIS EXAMPLE.
EVERYTHING 10% LESS THAN ANYWHERE ELSE
I THINK THIS IS IT.
KHALEDONYAHN CARPET FAKIR NO FAKES
KNOCK KNOCK KNOCK
HOOTS, MON. COME YE IN!*
HOOTS TO YOU, TOO, O KHALEDONYAHN. I'M THE GRAND VIZIER, AND WE COULD BE IN CAHOOTS.
I WON'T ASK YOU TO SIT DOWN. THAT STOOL HAS A DICEY LEG.
3

*KHALEDONYAHN WAS BORN IN THE NORTHERNMOST PART OF HIS COUNTRY AND SOMETIMES LAPSES INTO ITS DIALECT.

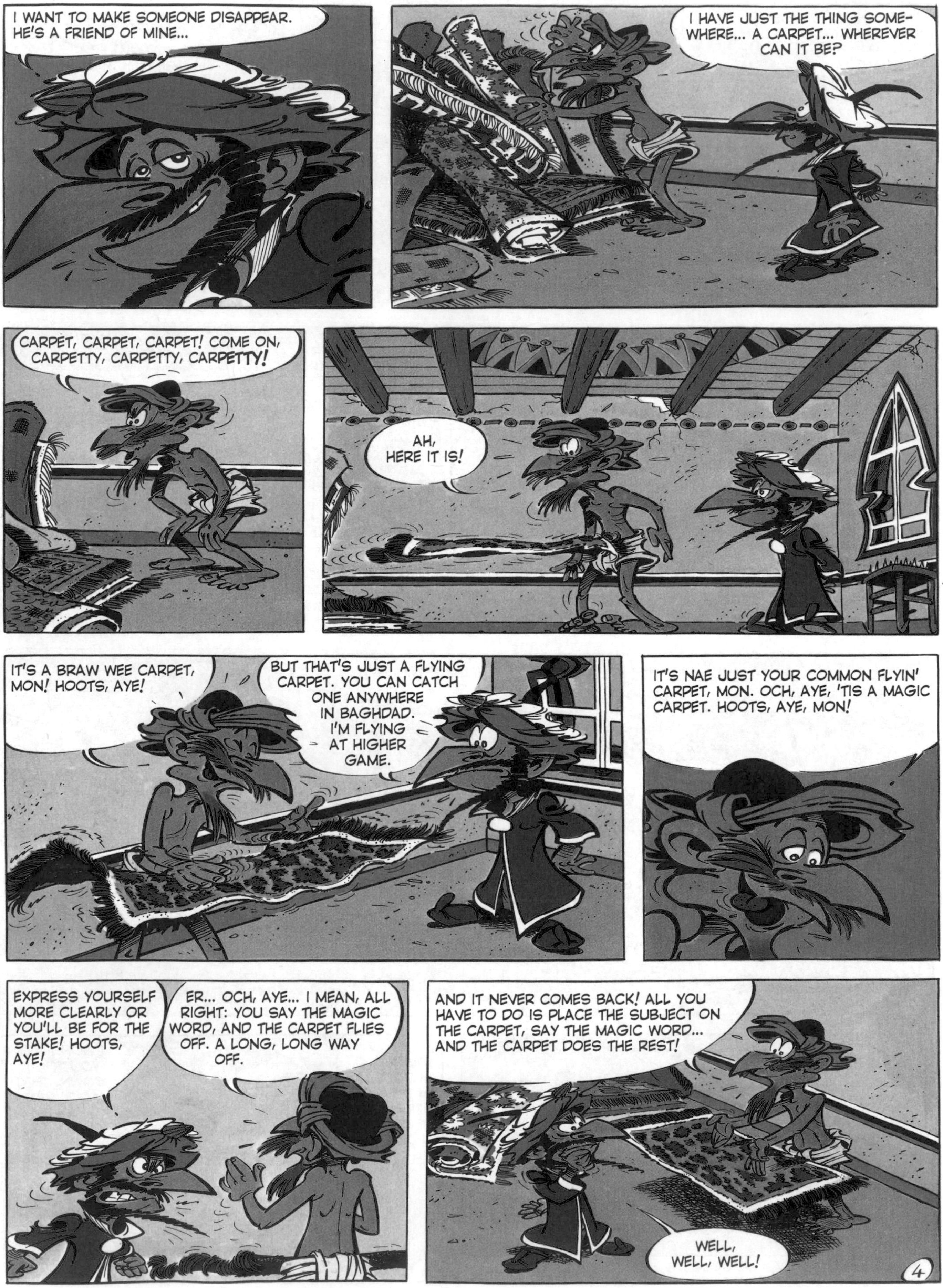
I WANT TO MAKE SOMEONE DISAPPEAR. HE'S A FRIEND OF MINE...
I HAVE JUST THE THING SOMEWHERE... A CARPET... WHEREVER CAN IT BE?
CARPET, CARPET, CARPET! COME ON, CARPETTY, CARPETTY, CARPETTY!
AH, HERE IT IS!
IT'S A BRAW WEE CARPET, MON! HOOTS, AYE!
BUT THAT'S JUST A FLYING CARPET. YOU CAN CATCH ONE ANYWHERE IN BAGHDAD. I'M FLYING AT HIGHER GAME.
IT'S NAE JUST YOUR COMMON FLYIN' CARPET, MON. OCH, AYE, 'TIS A MAGIC CARPET. HOOTS, AYE, MON!
EXPRESS YOURSELF MORE CLEARLY OR YOU'LL BE FOR THE STAKE! HOOTS, AYE!
ER... OCH, AYE... I MEAN, ALL RIGHT: YOU SAY THE MAGIC WORD, AND THE CARPET FLIES OFF. A LONG, LONG WAY OFF.
AND IT NEVER COMES BACK! ALL YOU HAVE TO DO IS PLACE THE SUBJECT ON THE CARPET, SAY THE MAGIC WORD... AND THE CARPET DOES THE REST!
WELL, WELL, WELL!
4

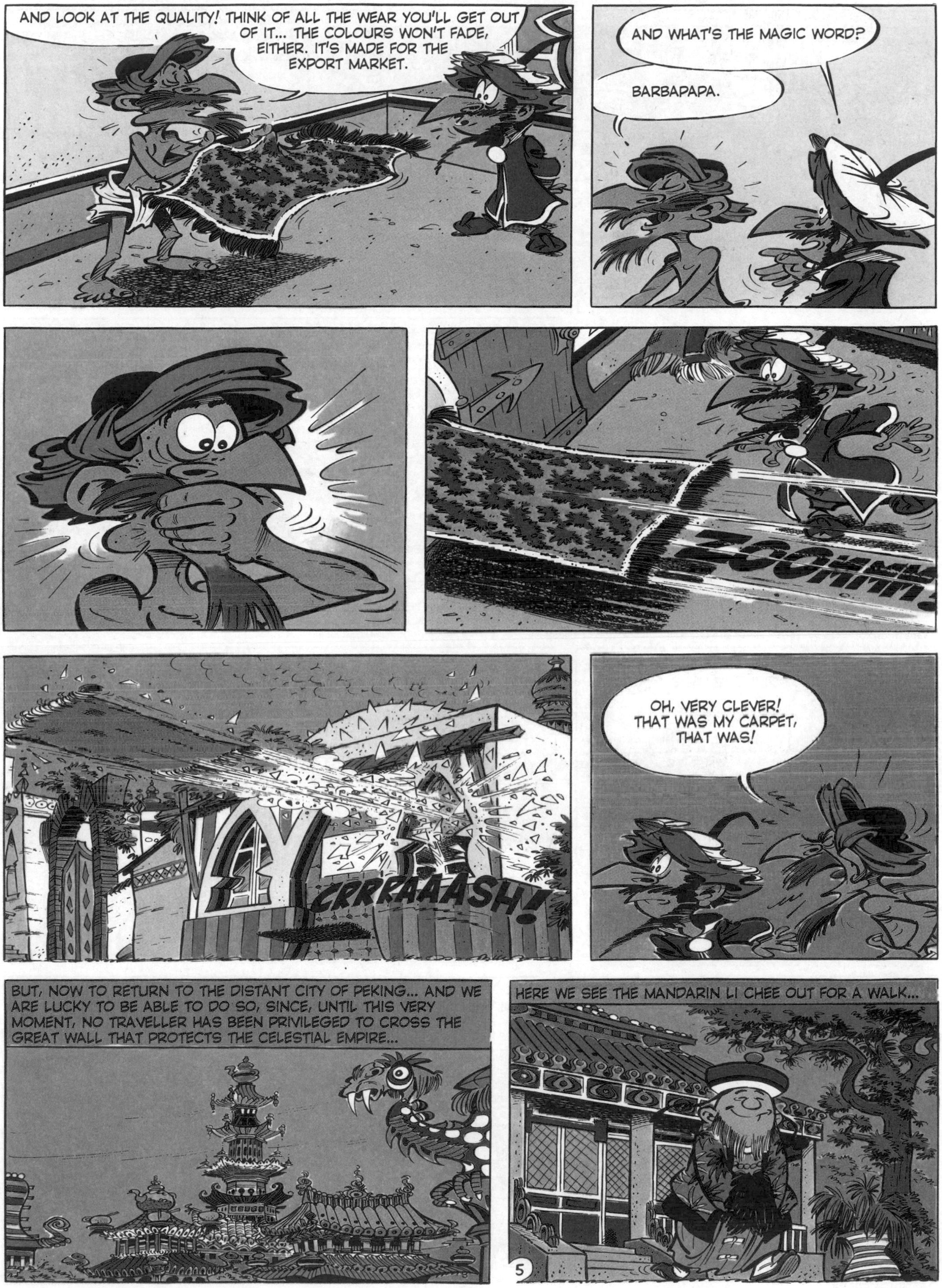

AND LOOK AT THE QUALITY! THINK OF ALL THE WEAR YOU'LL GET OUT OF IT... THE COLOURS WON'T FADE, EITHER. IT'S MADE FOR THE EXPORT MARKET.
AND WHAT'S THE MAGIC WORD?
BARBAPAPA.
ZOOMMM!
CRRRAAAASH!
OH, VERY CLEVER! THAT WAS MY CARPET, THAT WAS!
BUT, NOW TO RETURN TO THE DISTANT CITY OF PEKING... AND WE ARE LUCKY TO BE ABLE TO DO SO, SINCE, UNTIL THIS VERY MOMENT, NO TRAVELLER HAS BEEN PRIVILEGED TO CROSS THE GREAT WALL THAT PROTECTS THE CELESTIAL EMPIRE...
HERE WE SEE THE MANDARIN LI CHEE OUT FOR A WALK...
5

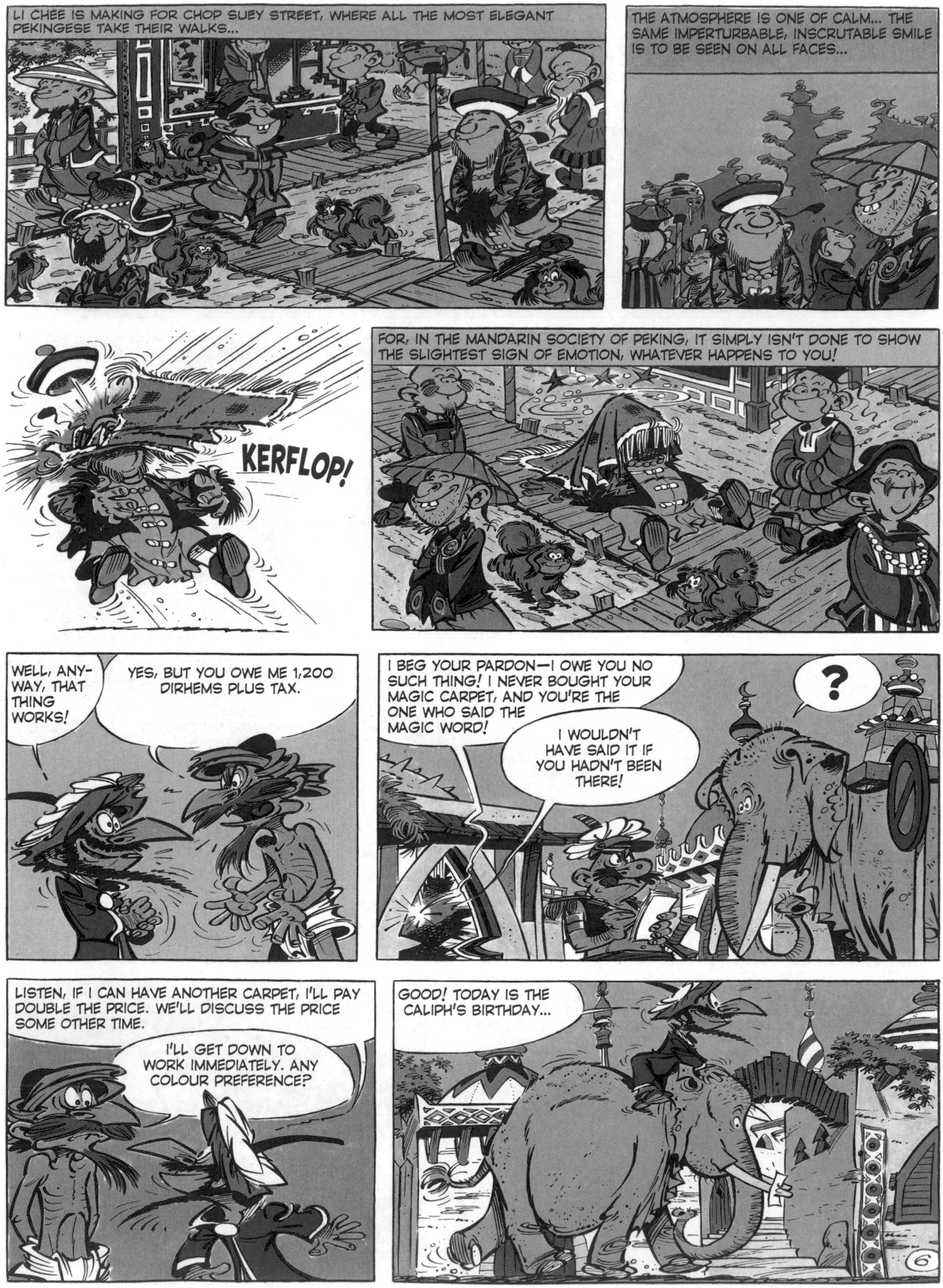

LI CHEE IS MAKING FOR CHOP SUEY STREET, WHERE ALL THE MOST ELEGANT PEKINGESE TAKE THEIR WALKS...
THE ATMOSPHERE IS ONE OF CALM... THE SAME IMPERTURBABLE, INSCRUTABLE SMILE IS TO BE SEEN ON ALL FACES...
KERFLOP!
FOR, IN THE MANDARIN SOCIETY OF PEKING, IT SIMPLY ISN'T DONE TO SHOW THE SLIGHTEST SIGN OF EMOTION, WHATEVER HAPPENS TO YOU!
WELL, ANYWAY, THAT THING WORKS!
YES, BUT YOU OWE ME 1,200 DIRHEMS PLUS TAX.
I BEG YOUR PARDON—I OWE YOU NO SUCH THING! I NEVER BOUGHT YOUR MAGIC CARPET, AND YOU'RE THE ONE WHO SAID THE MAGIC WORD!
I WOULDN'T HAVE SAID IT IF YOU HADN'T BEEN THERE!
?
LISTEN, IF I CAN HAVE ANOTHER CARPET, I'LL PAY DOUBLE THE PRICE. WE'LL DISCUSS THE PRICE SOME OTHER TIME.
I'LL GET DOWN TO WORK IMMEDIATELY. ANY COLOUR PREFERENCE?
GOOD! TODAY IS THE CALIPH'S BIRTHDAY...
6

... SO, NOW, TO PUT HIM ON THE MAT!
IZNOGOUD! YOU'VE COME TO WISH ME MANY HAPPY RETURNS!
NOT EXACTLY, O COMMANDER OF THE FAITHFUL. I'VE BEEN OUT BUYING YOU A WONDERFUL SURPRISE PRESENT!
A PRESENT? A SURPRISE PRESENT? WHATEVER CAN IT BE? DO TELL ME!
YOU'LL GET CARRIED AWAY...
A CARPET?
A CARPET.
BUT I ALREADY HAVE CARPETS. ANY NUMBER OF CARPETS. WALL-TO-WALL CARPETS! I WAS THINKING OF REPLACING THEM WITH VINYL CUSHION FLOORING, WHICH IS EASY TO KEEP CLEAN AND...
YOU'RE GOING TO GET A CARPET! WHETHER YOU LIKE IT OR NOT, YOU'RE GOING TO BE WELL AND TRULY CARPETED!
REALLY, THERE'S NO PLEASING SOME PEOPLE!
A FEW DAYS LATER...
I'M DELIVERING SOMETHING TO THE GRAND VIZIER.
OTHER END OF THE COURTYARD, STAIRCASE A, DOOR 18.
HERE YOU GO!
EXCELLENT!
7

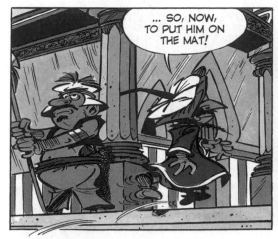

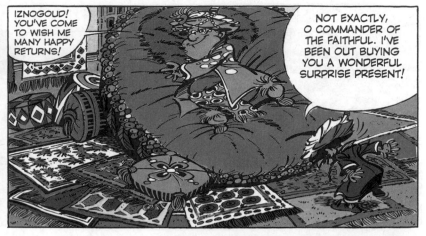

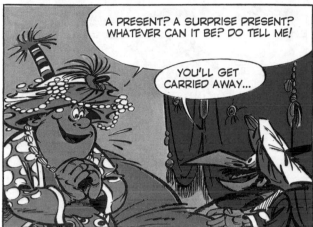

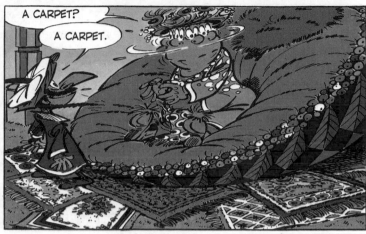

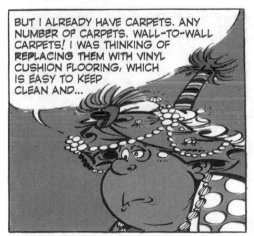

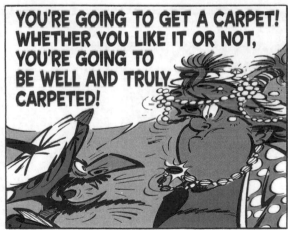

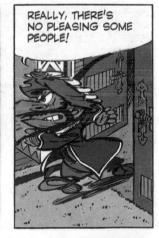

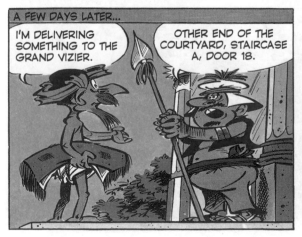

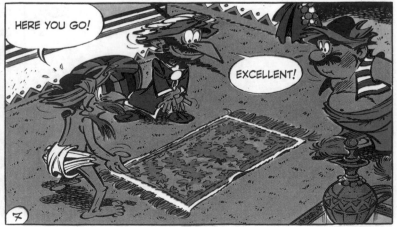

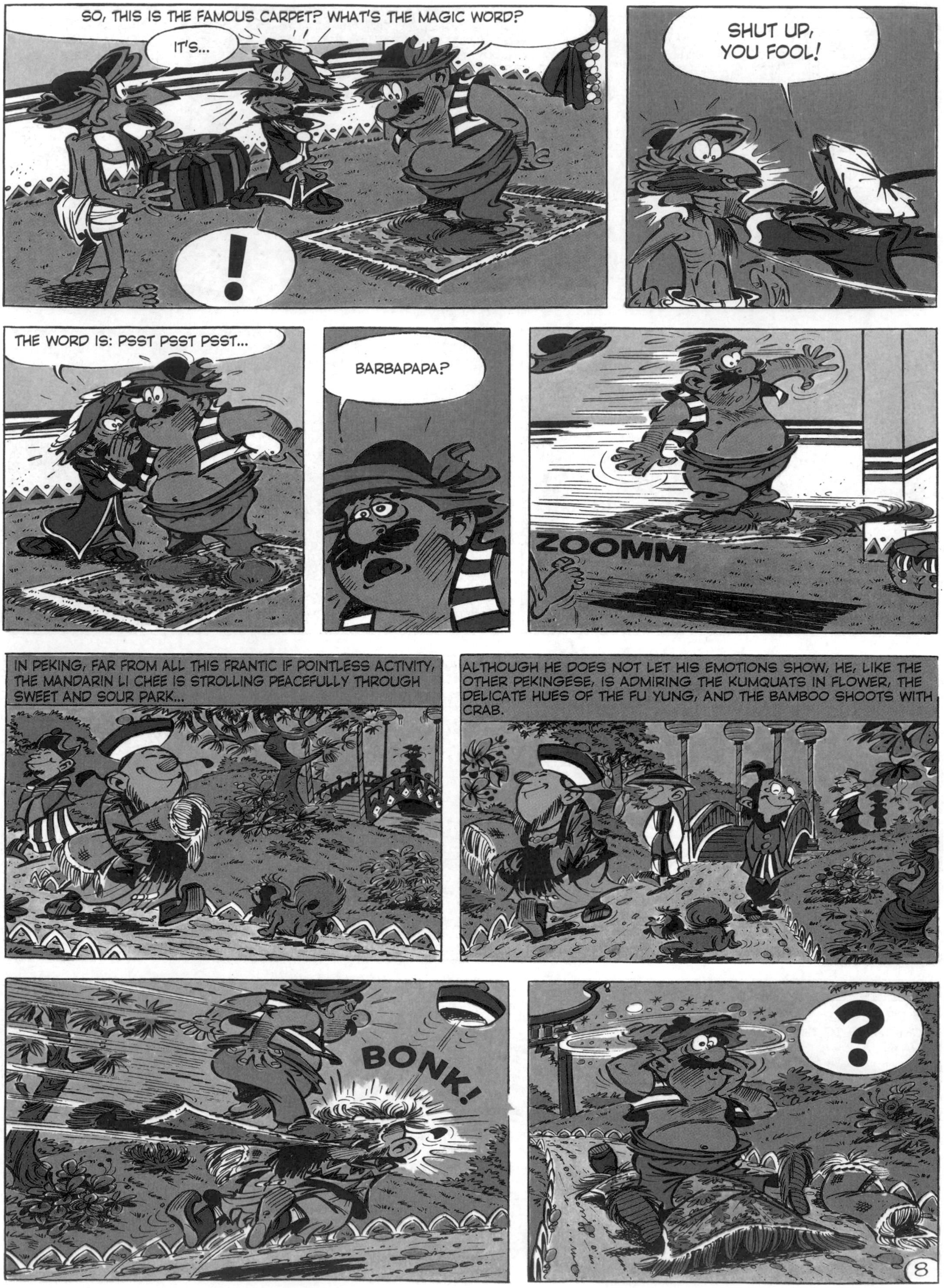
SO, THIS IS THE FAMOUS CARPET? WHAT'S THE MAGIC WORD?
IT'S...
!
SHUT UP, YOU FOOL!
THE WORD IS: PSST PSST PSST...
BARBAPAPA?
ZOOMM
IN PEKING, FAR FROM ALL THIS FRANTIC IF POINTLESS ACTIVITY, THE MANDARIN LI CHEE IS STROLLING PEACEFULLY THROUGH SWEET AND SOUR PARK...
ALTHOUGH HE DOES NOT LET HIS EMOTIONS SHOW, HE, LIKE THE OTHER PEKINGESE, IS ADMIRING THE KUMQUATS IN FLOWER, THE DELICATE HUES OF THE FU YUNG, AND THE BAMBOO SHOOTS WITH CRAB.
BONK!
?
8

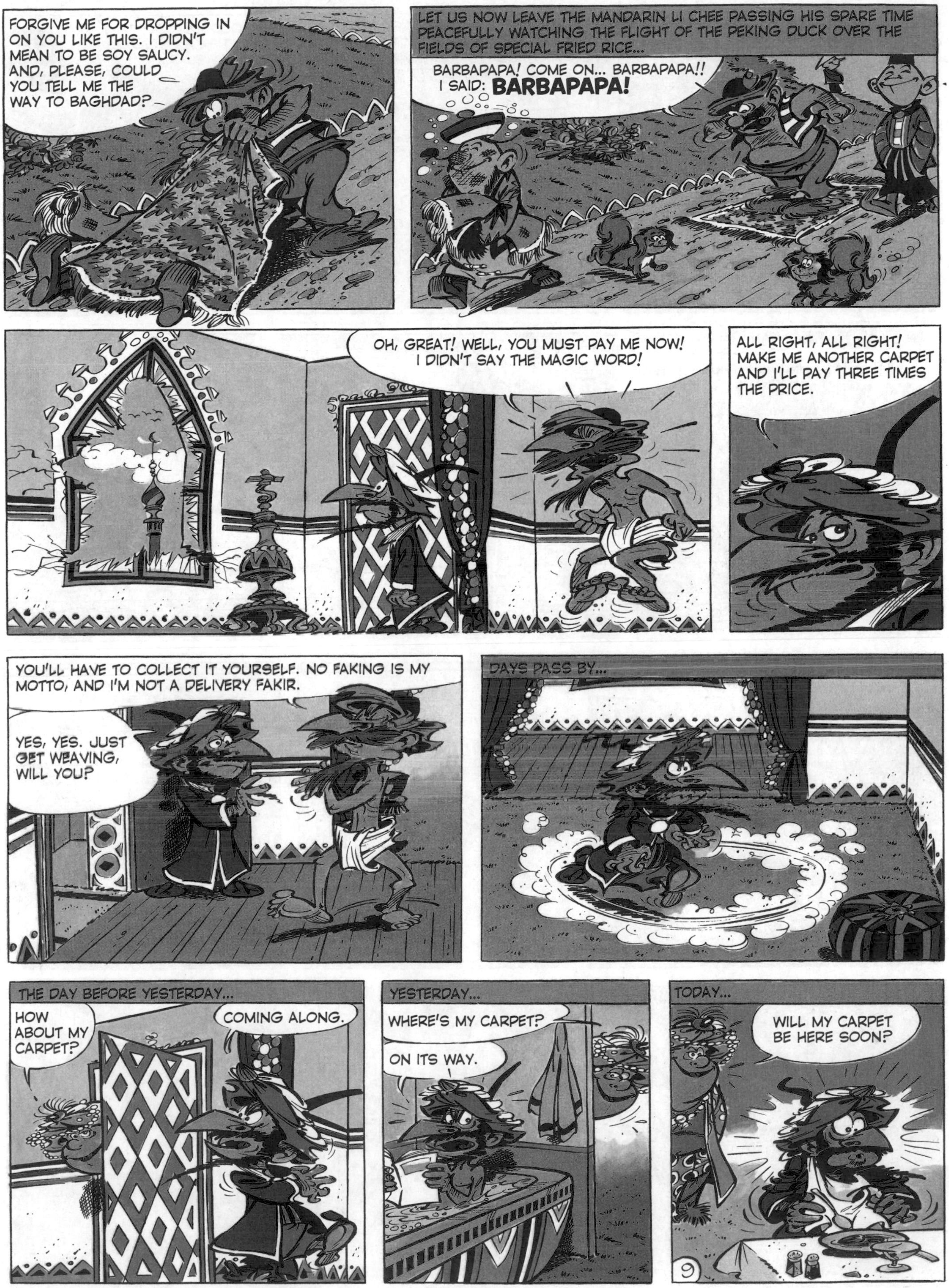
FORGIVE ME FOR DROPPING IN ON YOU LIKE THIS. I DIDN'T MEAN TO BE SOY SAUCY. AND, PLEASE, COULD YOU TELL ME THE WAY TO BAGHDAD?
LET US NOW LEAVE THE MANDARIN LI CHEE PASSING HIS SPARE TIME PEACEFULLY WATCHING THE FLIGHT OF THE PEKING DUCK OVER THE FIELDS OF SPECIAL FRIED RICE...
BARBAPAPA! COME ON... BARBAPAPA!! I SAID: BARBAPAPA!
OH, GREAT! WELL, YOU MUST PAY ME NOW! I DIDN'T SAY THE MAGIC WORD!
ALL RIGHT, ALL RIGHT! MAKE ME ANOTHER CARPET AND I'LL PAY THREE TIMES THE PRICE.
YOU'LL HAVE TO COLLECT IT YOURSELF. NO FAKING IS MY MOTTO, AND I'M NOT A DELIVERY FAKIR.
YES, YES. JUST GET WEAVING, WILL YOU?
DAYS PASS BY...
THE DAY BEFORE YESTERDAY...
HOW ABOUT MY CARPET?
COMING ALONG.
YESTERDAY...
WHERE'S MY CARPET?
ON ITS WAY.
TODAY...
WILL MY CARPET BE HERE SOON?

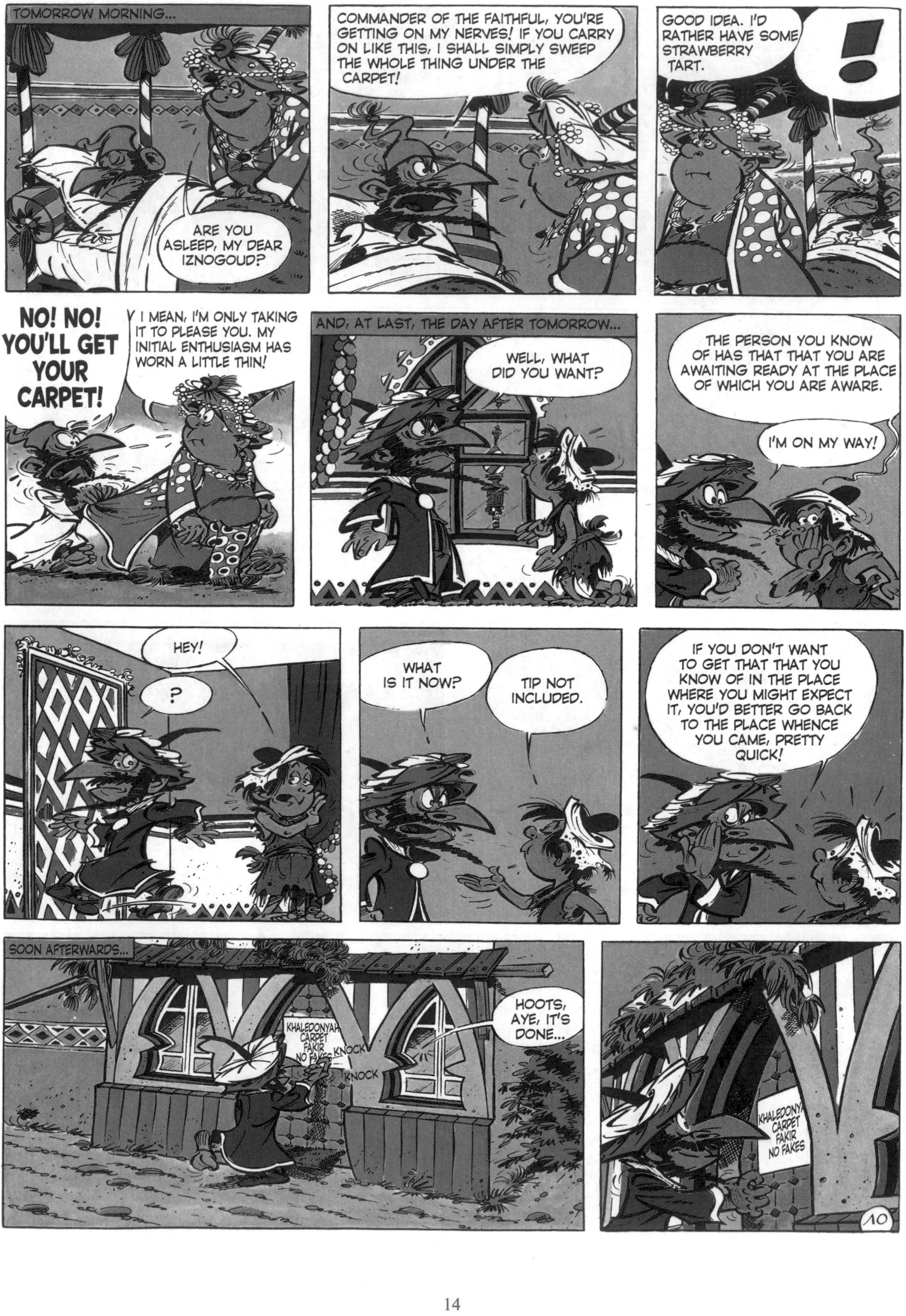
TOMORROW MORNING...
ARE YOU ASLEEP, MY DEAR IZNOGOUD?
COMMANDER OF THE FAITHFUL, YOU'RE GETTING ON MY NERVES! IF YOU CARRY ON LIKE THIS, I SHALL SIMPLY SWEEP THE WHOLE THING UNDER THE CARPET!
GOOD IDEA. I'D RATHER HAVE SOME STRAWBERRY TART.
!
NO! NO! YOU'LL GET YOUR CARPET!
I MEAN, I'M ONLY TAKING IT TO PLEASE YOU. MY INITIAL ENTHUSIASM HAS WORN A LITTLE THIN!
AND, AT LAST, THE DAY AFTER TOMORROW...
WELL, WHAT DID YOU WANT?
THE PERSON YOU KNOW OF HAS THAT THAT YOU ARE AWAITING READY AT THE PLACE OF WHICH YOU ARE AWARE.
I'M ON MY WAY!
HEY!
?
WHAT IS IT NOW?
TIP NOT INCLUDED.
IF YOU DON'T WANT TO GET THAT THAT YOU KNOW OF IN THE PLACE WHERE YOU MIGHT EXPECT IT, YOU'D BETTER GO BACK TO THE PLACE WHENCE YOU CAME, PRETTY QUICK!
SOON AFTERWARDS...
KHALEDONYAH CARPET FAKIR NO FAKES
KNOCK
KNOCK
HOOTS, AYE, IT'S DONE...
KHALEDONYA CARPET FAKIR NO FAKES
10

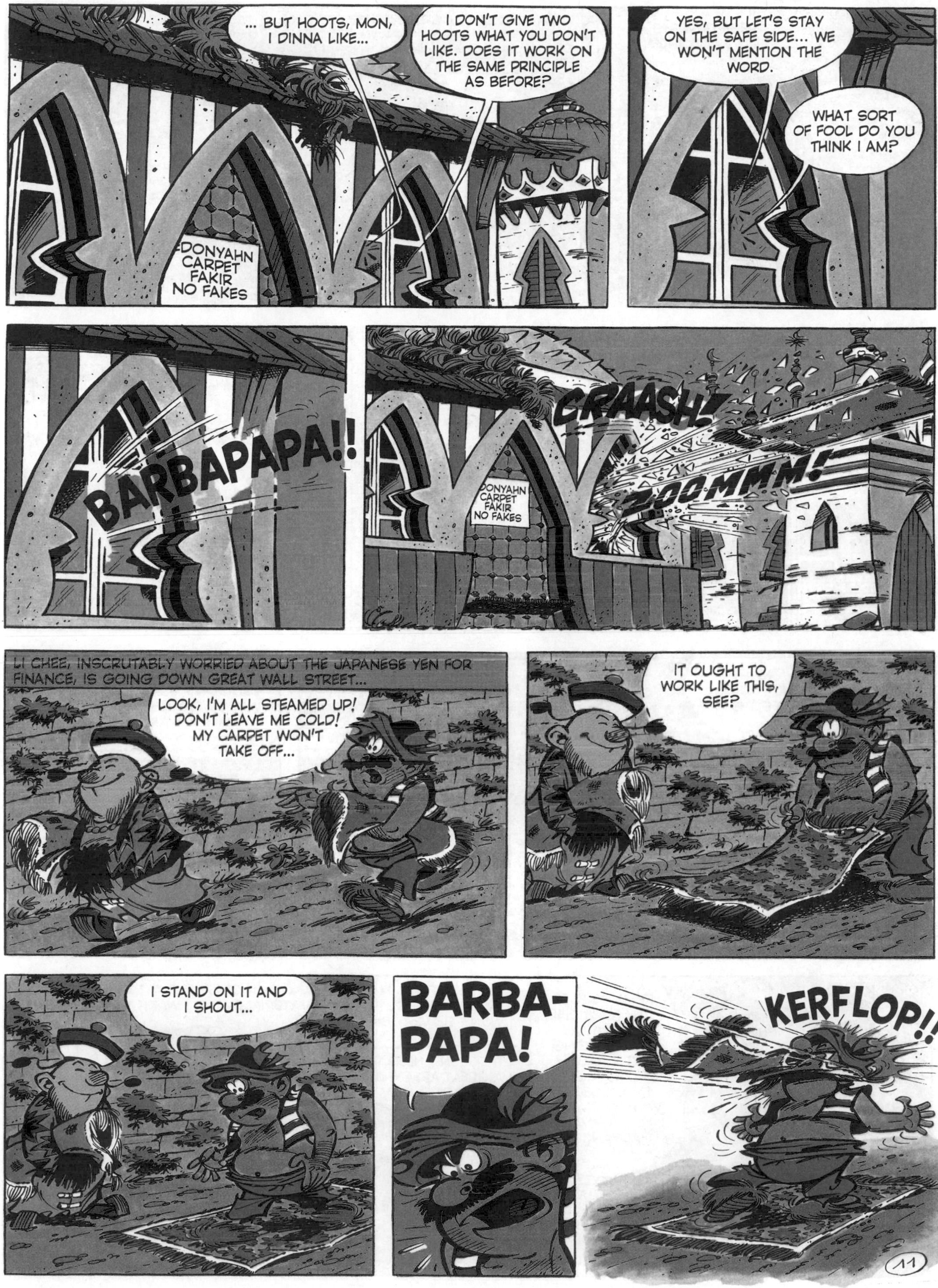
... BUT HOOTS, MON, I DINNA LIKE...
I DON'T GIVE TWO HOOTS WHAT YOU DON'T LIKE. DOES IT WORK ON THE SAME PRINCIPLE AS BEFORE?
DONYAHN CARPET FAKIR NO FAKES
YES, BUT LET'S STAY ON THE SAFE SIDE... WE WON'T MENTION THE WORD.
WHAT SORT OF FOOL DO YOU THINK I AM?
BARBAPAPA!!
CRAASH!
ZOOMMM!
DONYAHN CARPET FAKIR NO FAKES
LI CHEE, INSCRUTABLY WORRIED ABOUT THE JAPANESE YEN FOR FINANCE, IS GOING DOWN GREAT WALL STREET...
LOOK, I'M ALL STEAMED UP! DON'T LEAVE ME COLD! MY CARPET WON'T TAKE OFF...
IT OUGHT TO WORK LIKE THIS, SEE?
I STAND ON IT AND I SHOUT...
BARBA-PAPA!
KERFLOP!!
11

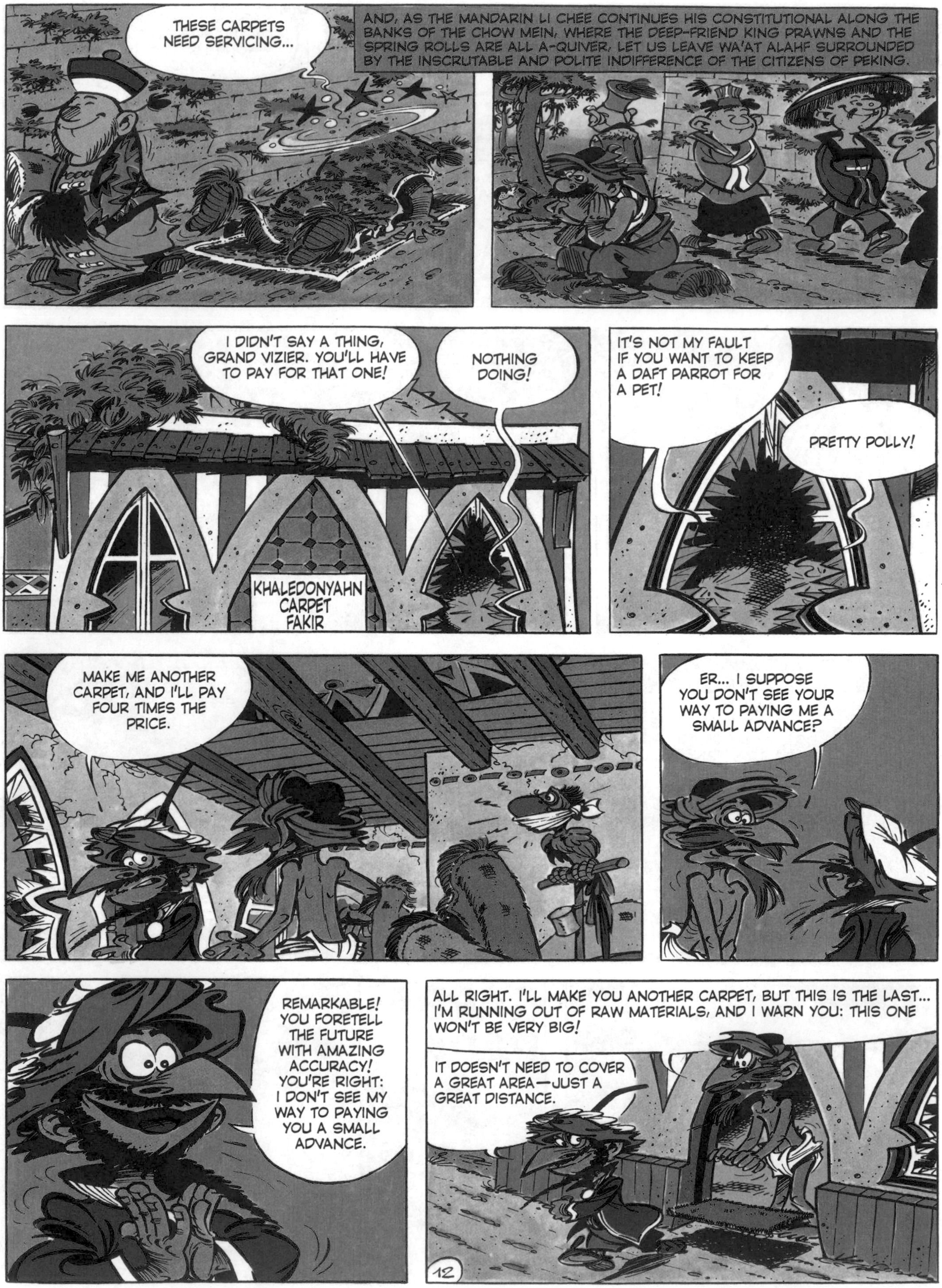
THESE CARPETS NEED SERVICING...
AND, AS THE MANDARIN LI CHEE CONTINUES HIS CONSTITUTIONAL ALONG THE BANKS OF THE CHOW MEIN, WHERE THE DEEP-FRIEND KING PRAWNS AND THE SPRING ROLLS ARE ALL A-QUIVER, LET US LEAVE WA'AT ALAHF SURROUNDED BY THE INSCRUTABLE AND POLITE INDIFFERENCE OF THE CITIZENS OF PEKING.
I DIDN'T SAY A THING, GRAND VIZIER. YOU'LL HAVE TO PAY FOR THAT ONE!
NOTHING DOING!
KHALEDONYAHN CARPET FAKIR
IT'S NOT MY FAULT IF YOU WANT TO KEEP A DAFT PARROT FOR A PET!
PRETTY POLLY!
MAKE ME ANOTHER CARPET, AND I'LL PAY FOUR TIMES THE PRICE.
ER... I SUPPOSE YOU DON'T SEE YOUR WAY TO PAYING ME A SMALL ADVANCE?
REMARKABLE! YOU FORETELL THE FUTURE WITH AMAZING ACCURACY! YOU'RE RIGHT: I DON'T SEE MY WAY TO PAYING YOU A SMALL ADVANCE.
ALL RIGHT. I'LL MAKE YOU ANOTHER CARPET, BUT THIS IS THE LAST... I'M RUNNING OUT OF RAW MATERIALS, AND I WARN YOU: THIS ONE WON'T BE VERY BIG!
IT DOESN'T NEED TO COVER A GREAT AREA—JUST A GREAT DISTANCE.
12

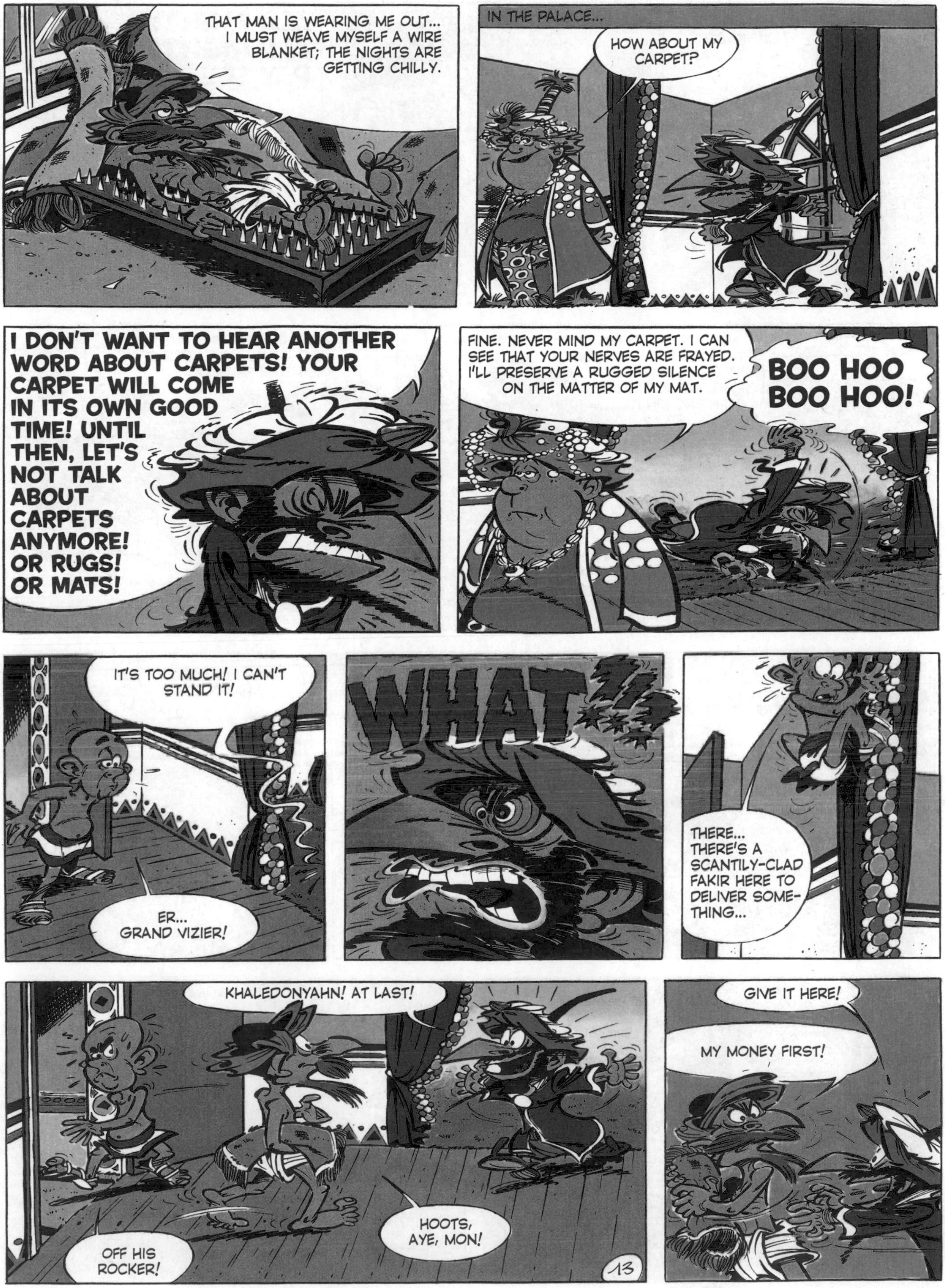
THAT MAN IS WEARING ME OUT... I MUST WEAVE MYSELF A WIRE BLANKET; THE NIGHTS ARE GETTING CHILLY.
IN THE PALACE...
HOW ABOUT MY CARPET?
I DON'T WANT TO HEAR ANOTHER WORD ABOUT CARPETS! YOUR CARPET WILL COME IN ITS OWN GOOD TIME! UNTIL THEN, LET'S NOT TALK ABOUT CARPETS ANYMORE! OR RUGS! OR MATS!
FINE. NEVER MIND MY CARPET. I CAN SEE THAT YOUR NERVES ARE FRAYED. I'LL PRESERVE A RUGGED SILENCE ON THE MATTER OF MY MAT.
BOO HOO BOO HOO!
IT'S TOO MUCH! I CAN'T STAND IT!
ER... GRAND VIZIER!
WHAT?!
THERE... THERE'S A SCANTILY-CLAD FAKIR HERE TO DELIVER SOME-THING...
KHALEDONYAHN! AT LAST!
HOOTS, AYE, MON!
OFF HIS ROCKER!
13
GIVE IT HERE!
MY MONEY FIRST!

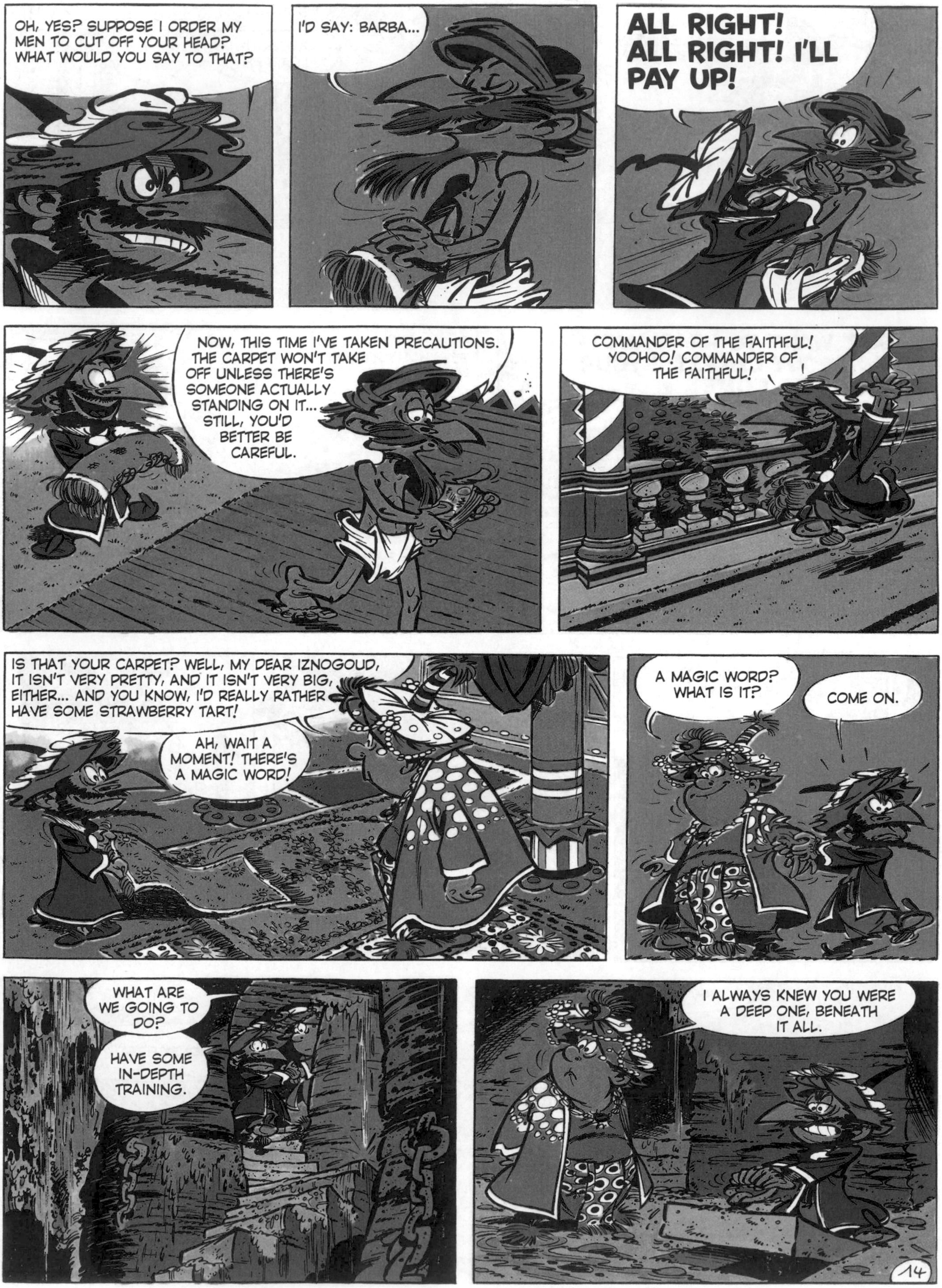
OH, YES? SUPPOSE I ORDER MY MEN TO CUT OFF YOUR HEAD? WHAT WOULD YOU SAY TO THAT?
I'D SAY: BARBA...
ALL RIGHT! ALL RIGHT! I'LL PAY UP!
NOW, THIS TIME I'VE TAKEN PRECAUTIONS. THE CARPET WON'T TAKE OFF UNLESS THERE'S SOMEONE ACTUALLY STANDING ON IT... STILL, YOU'D BETTER BE CAREFUL.
COMMANDER OF THE FAITHFUL! YOOHOO! COMMANDER OF THE FAITHFUL!
IS THAT YOUR CARPET? WELL, MY DEAR IZNOGOUD, IT ISN'T VERY PRETTY, AND IT ISN'T VERY BIG, EITHER... AND YOU KNOW, I'D REALLY RATHER HAVE SOME STRAWBERRY TART!
AH, WAIT A MOMENT! THERE'S A MAGIC WORD!
A MAGIC WORD? WHAT IS IT?
COME ON.
WHAT ARE WE GOING TO DO?
HAVE SOME IN-DEPTH TRAINING.
I ALWAYS KNEW YOU WERE A DEEP ONE, BENEATH IT ALL.
14

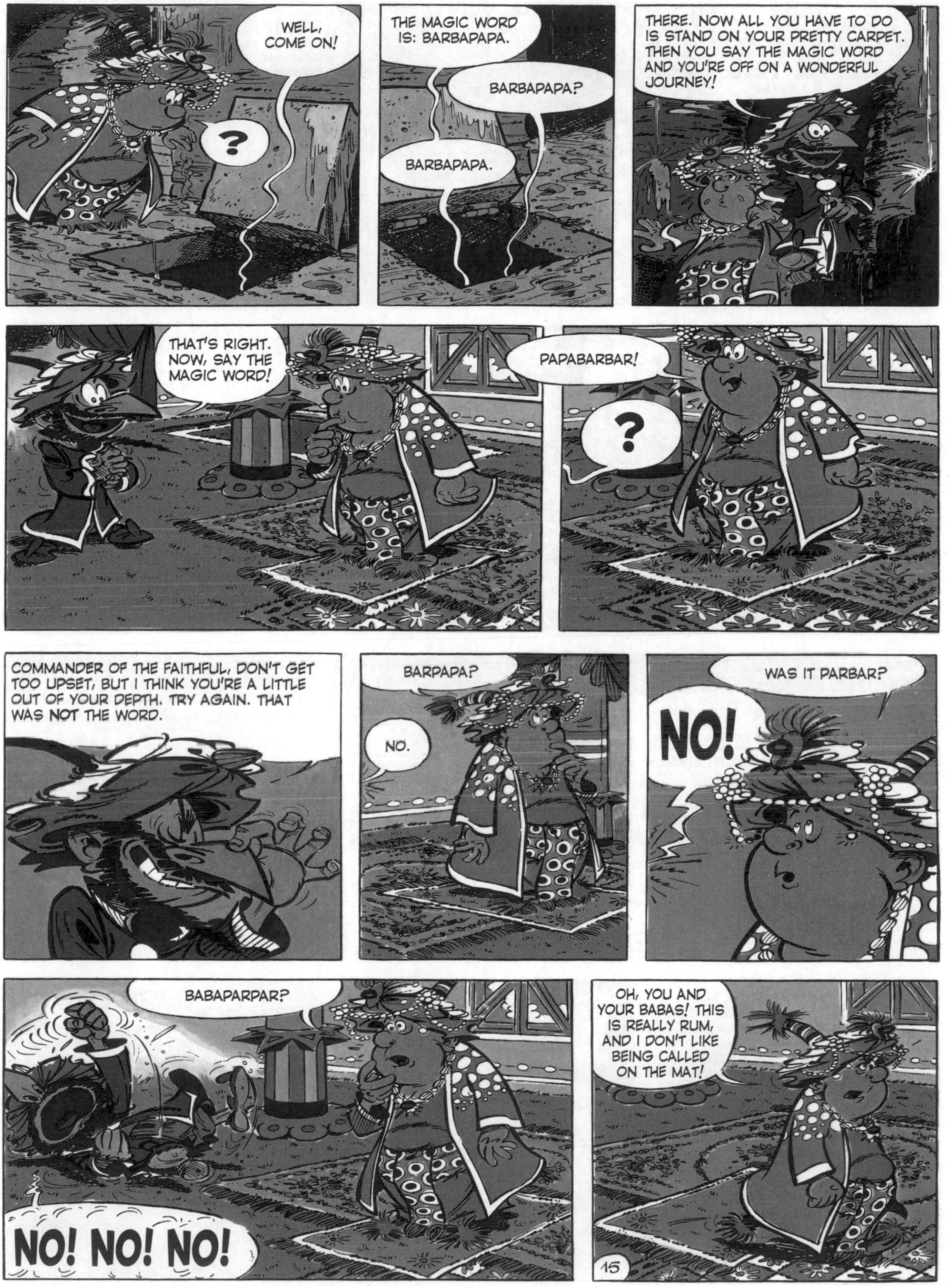
WELL, COME ON!
?
THE MAGIC WORD IS: BARBAPAPA.
BARBAPAPA?
BARBAPAPA.
THERE. NOW ALL YOU HAVE TO DO IS STAND ON YOUR PRETTY CARPET. THEN YOU SAY THE MAGIC WORD AND YOU'RE OFF ON A WONDERFUL JOURNEY!
THAT'S RIGHT. NOW, SAY THE MAGIC WORD!
PAPABARBAR!
?
COMMANDER OF THE FAITHFUL, DON'T GET TOO UPSET, BUT I THINK YOU'RE A LITTLE OUT OF YOUR DEPTH. TRY AGAIN. THAT WAS NOT THE WORD.
BARPAPA?
NO.
WAS IT PARBAR?
NO!
BABAPARPAR?
NO! NO! NO!
OH, YOU AND YOUR BABAS! THIS IS REALLY RUM, AND I DON'T LIKE BEING CALLED ON THE MAT!
15

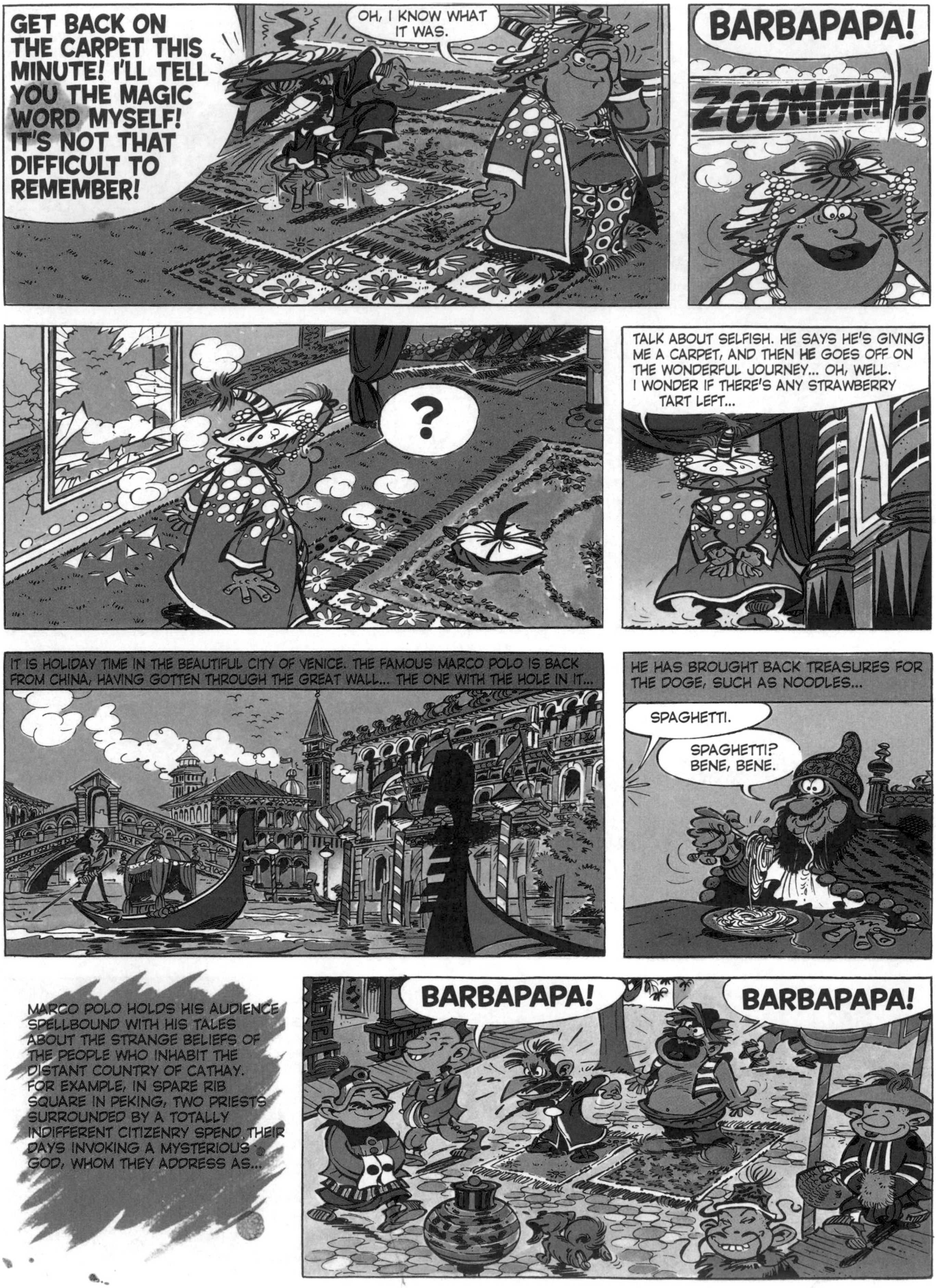
GET BACK ON THE CARPET THIS MINUTE! I'LL TELL YOU THE MAGIC WORD MYSELF! IT'S NOT THAT DIFFICULT TO REMEMBER!
OH, I KNOW WHAT IT WAS.
BARBAPAPA!
ZOOMMMM!
?
TALK ABOUT SELFISH. HE SAYS HE'S GIVING ME A CARPET, AND THEN HE GOES OFF ON THE WONDERFUL JOURNEY... OH, WELL. I WONDER IF THERE'S ANY STRAWBERRY TART LEFT...
IT IS HOLIDAY TIME IN THE BEAUTIFUL CITY OF VENICE. THE FAMOUS MARCO POLO IS BACK FROM CHINA, HAVING GOTTEN THROUGH THE GREAT WALL... THE ONE WITH THE HOLE IN IT...
HE HAS BROUGHT BACK TREASURES FOR THE DOGE, SUCH AS NOODLES...
SPAGHETTI.
SPAGHETTI!? BENE, BENE.
MARCO POLO HOLDS HIS AUDIENCE SPELLBOUND WITH HIS TALES ABOUT THE STRANGE BELIEFS OF THE PEOPLE WHO INHABIT THE DISTANT COUNTRY OF CATHAY. FOR EXAMPLE, IN SPARE RIB SQUARE IN PEKING, TWO PRIESTS SURROUNDED BY A TOTALLY INDIFFERENT CITIZENRY SPEND THEIR DAYS INVOKING A MYSTERIOUS GOD, WHOM THEY ADDRESS AS...
BARBAPAPA!
BARBAPAPA!

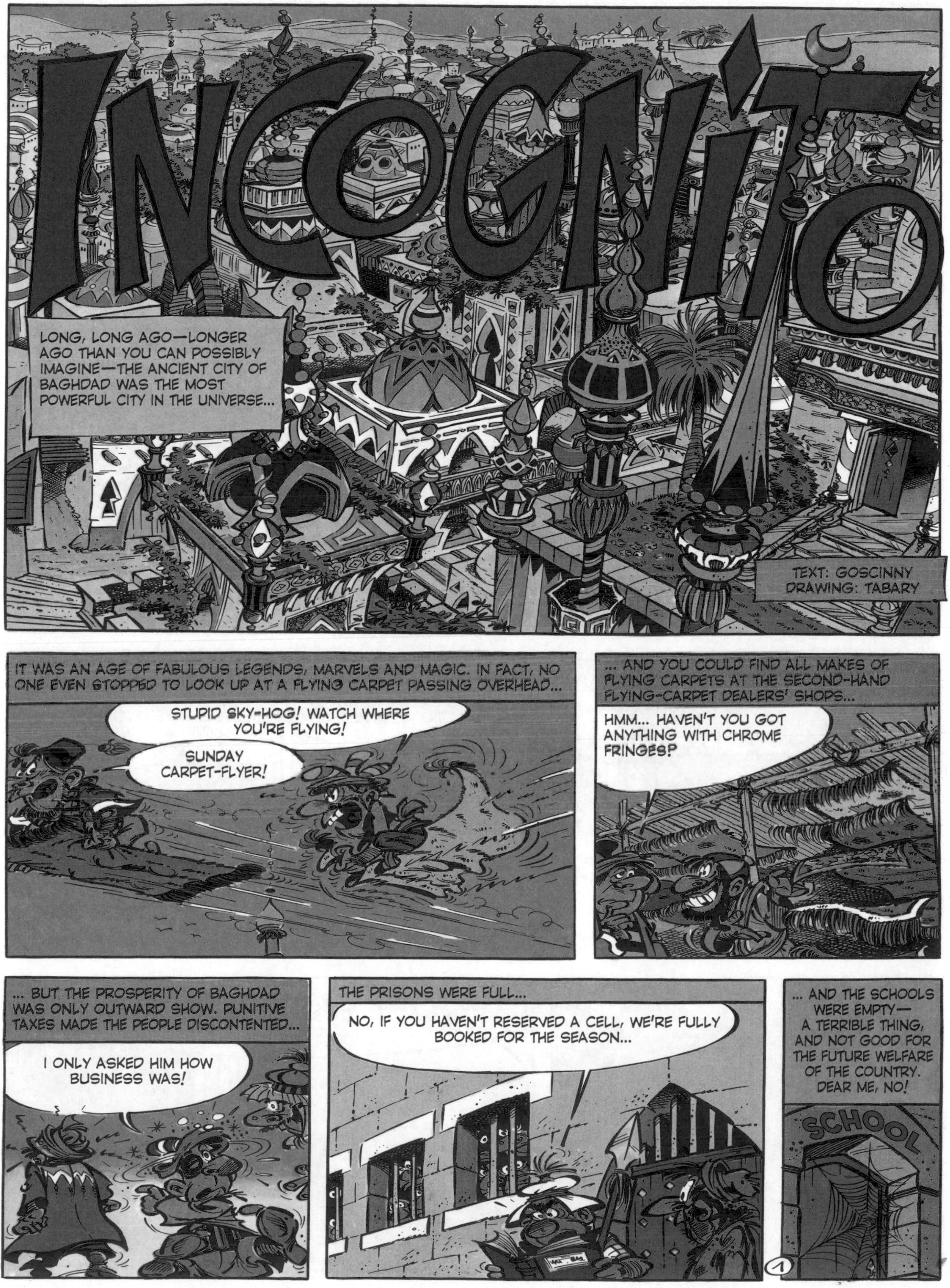
INCOGNITO
LONG, LONG AGO—LONGER AGO THAN YOU CAN POSSIBLY IMAGINE—THE ANCIENT CITY OF BAGHDAD WAS THE MOST POWERFUL CITY IN THE UNIVERSE...
TEXT: GOSCINNY
DRAWING: TABARY
IT WAS AN AGE OF FABULOUS LEGENDS, MARVELS AND MAGIC. IN FACT, NO ONE EVEN STOPPED TO LOOK UP AT A FLYING CARPET PASSING OVERHEAD...
STUPID SKY-HOG! WATCH WHERE YOU'RE FLYING!
SUNDAY CARPET-FLYER!
... AND YOU COULD FIND ALL MAKES OF FLYING CARPETS AT THE SECOND-HAND FLYING-CARPET DEALERS' SHOPS...
HMM... HAVEN'T YOU GOT ANYTHING WITH CHROME FRINGES?
... BUT THE PROSPERITY OF BAGHDAD WAS ONLY OUTWARD SHOW. PUNITIVE TAXES MADE THE PEOPLE DISCONTENTED...
I ONLY ASKED HIM HOW BUSINESS WAS!
THE PRISONS WERE FULL...
NO, IF YOU HAVEN'T RESERVED A CELL, WE'RE FULLY BOOKED FOR THE SEASON...
... AND THE SCHOOLS WERE EMPTY— A TERRIBLE THING, AND NOT GOOD FOR THE FUTURE WELFARE OF THE COUNTRY. DEAR ME, NO!
SCHOOL
1

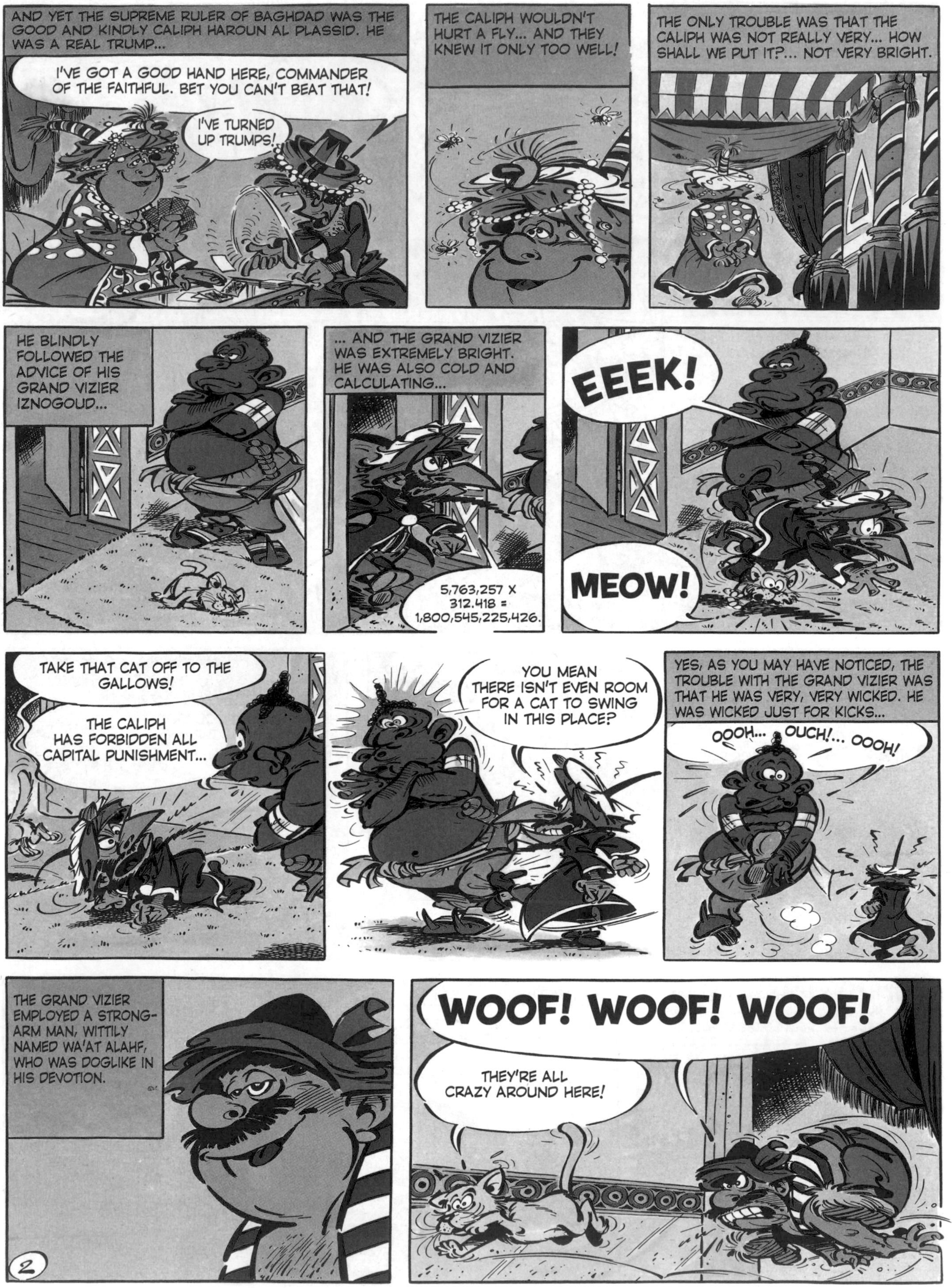
AND YET THE SUPREME RULER OF BAGHDAD WAS THE GOOD AND KINDLY CALIPH HAROUN AL PLASSID. HE WAS A REAL TRUMP...
I'VE GOT A GOOD HAND HERE, COMMANDER OF THE FAITHFUL. BET YOU CAN'T BEAT THAT!
I'VE TURNED UP TRUMPS!
THE CALIPH WOULDN'T HURT A FLY... AND THEY KNEW IT ONLY TOO WELL!
THE ONLY TROUBLE WAS THAT THE CALIPH WAS NOT REALLY VERY... HOW SHALL WE PUT IT?... NOT VERY BRIGHT.
HE BLINDLY FOLLOWED THE ADVICE OF HIS GRAND VIZIER IZNOGOUD...
... AND THE GRAND VIZIER WAS EXTREMELY BRIGHT. HE WAS ALSO COLD AND CALCULATING...
5,763,257 X 312.418 = 1,800,545,225,426.
EEEK!
MEOW!
TAKE THAT CAT OFF TO THE GALLOWS!
THE CALIPH HAS FORBIDDEN ALL CAPITAL PUNISHMENT...
YOU MEAN THERE ISN'T EVEN ROOM FOR A CAT TO SWING IN THIS PLACE?
YES, AS YOU MAY HAVE NOTICED, THE TROUBLE WITH THE GRAND VIZIER WAS THAT HE WAS VERY, VERY WICKED. HE WAS WICKED JUST FOR KICKS...
OOOH... OUCH!... OOOH!
THE GRAND VIZIER EMPLOYED A STRONG-ARM MAN, WITTILY NAMED WA'AT ALAHF, WHO WAS DOGLIKE IN HIS DEVOTION.
2
WOOF! WOOF! WOOF!
THEY'RE ALL CRAZY AROUND HERE!

THE CALIPH'S GOODNESS OF HEART INFURIATED THE GRAND VIZIER...

... FOR, AS WE WERE SAYING, THE GRAND VIZIER WAS VERY WICKED... AND, WOULD YOU BELIEVE IT, HIS AMBITION WAS TO BECOME CALIPH INSTEAD OF THE CALIPH HIMSELF!

THANK GOODNESS THE CALIPH ALWAYS FOLLOWS MY ADVICE...

... AND WILL SIGN DECREES IMPOSING CRUSHING TAXATION AND PUNISHING WITH IMPRISONMENT ANYONE WHO WON'T PAY UP!

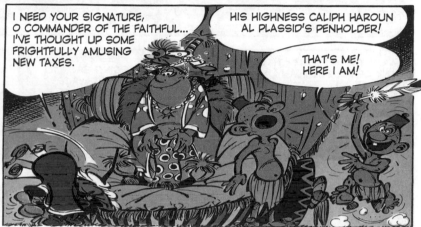

I NEED YOUR SIGNATURE, O COMMANDER OF THE FAITHFUL... I'VE THOUGHT UP SOME FRIGHTFULLY AMUSING NEW TAXES.

HIS HIGHNESS CALIPH HAROUN AL PLASSID'S PENHOLDER!

THAT'S ME! HERE I AM!

MY DEAR IZNOGOUD, I FEEL LIKE GOING OUT INTO THE STREETS OF BAGHDAD TO DISCOVER WHAT MY PEOPLE REALLY THINK OF ME.

THE CALIPH WISHES TO MINGLE WITH HIS SUBJECTS! PREPARE FOR HIS OUTING!

AND SOON AFTERWARDS, IN THE STREETS OF BAGHDAD...

THE CALIPH'S GUARDS! HIDE YOURSELVES!

YES, THIS IS HEADY NEWS FOR THE PEOPLE...

THE CALIPH IS ABOUT TO RIDE THROUGH THE STREETS, AND ANYONE WHO DARES SET EYES ON HIM WILL BE BEHEADED!

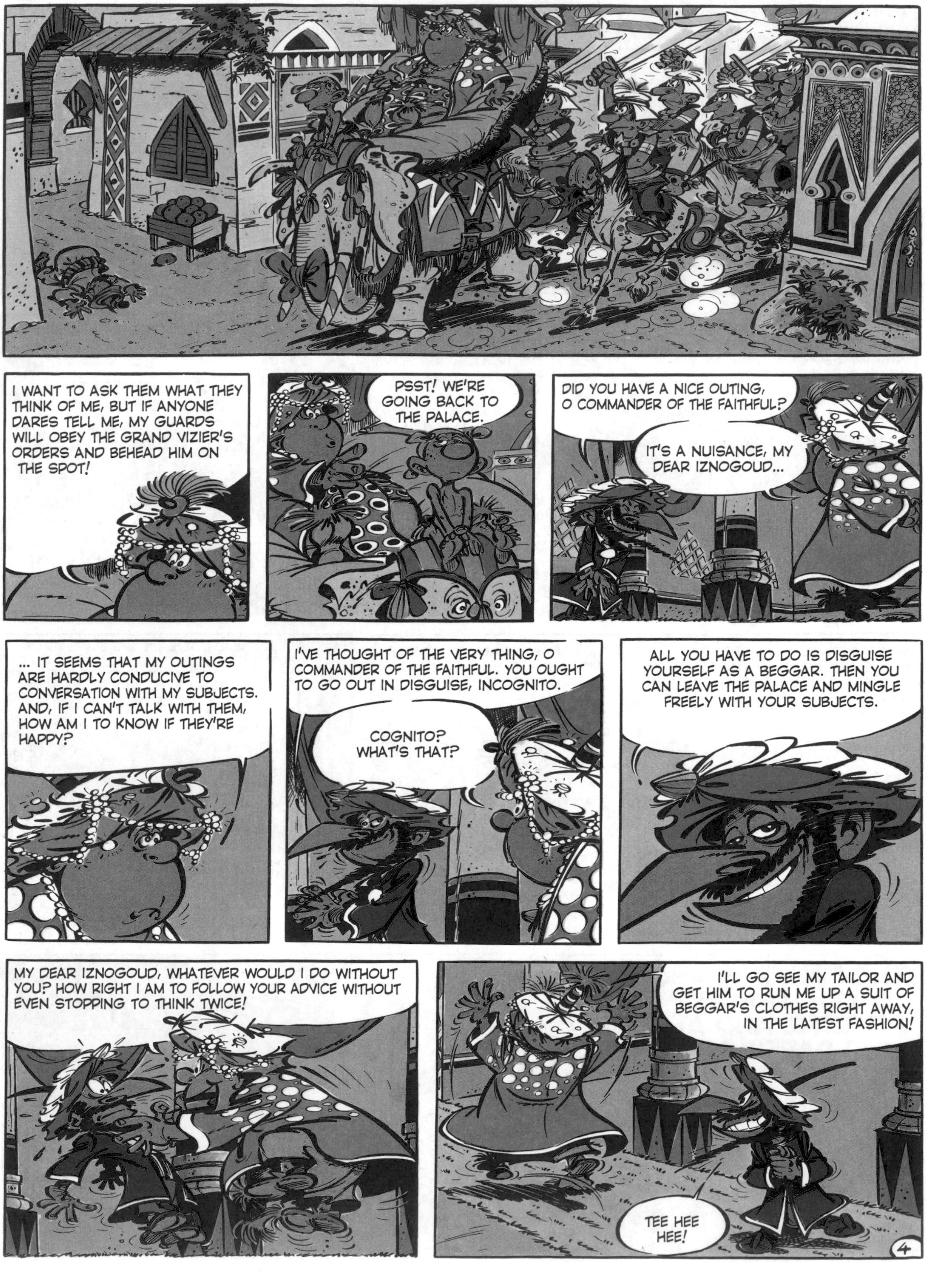
I WANT TO ASK THEM WHAT THEY THINK OF ME, BUT IF ANYONE DARES TELL ME, MY GUARDS WILL OBEY THE GRAND VIZIER'S ORDERS AND BEHEAD HIM ON THE SPOT!
PSST! WE'RE GOING BACK TO THE PALACE.
DID YOU HAVE A NICE OUTING, O COMMANDER OF THE FAITHFUL?
IT'S A NUISANCE, MY DEAR IZNOGOUD...
... IT SEEMS THAT MY OUTINGS ARE HARDLY CONDUCIVE TO CONVERSATION WITH MY SUBJECTS. AND, IF I CAN'T TALK WITH THEM, HOW AM I TO KNOW IF THEY'RE HAPPY?
I'VE THOUGHT OF THE VERY THING, O COMMANDER OF THE FAITHFUL. YOU OUGHT TO GO OUT IN DISGUISE, INCOGNITO.
COGNITO? WHAT'S THAT?
ALL YOU HAVE TO DO IS DISGUISE YOURSELF AS A BEGGAR. THEN YOU CAN LEAVE THE PALACE AND MINGLE FREELY WITH YOUR SUBJECTS.
MY DEAR IZNOGOUD, WHATEVER WOULD I DO WITHOUT YOU? HOW RIGHT I AM TO FOLLOW YOUR ADVICE WITHOUT EVEN STOPPING TO THINK TWICE!
I'LL GO SEE MY TAILOR AND GET HIM TO RUN ME UP A SUIT OF BEGGAR'S CLOTHES RIGHT AWAY, IN THE LATEST FASHION!
TEE HEE HEE!
4

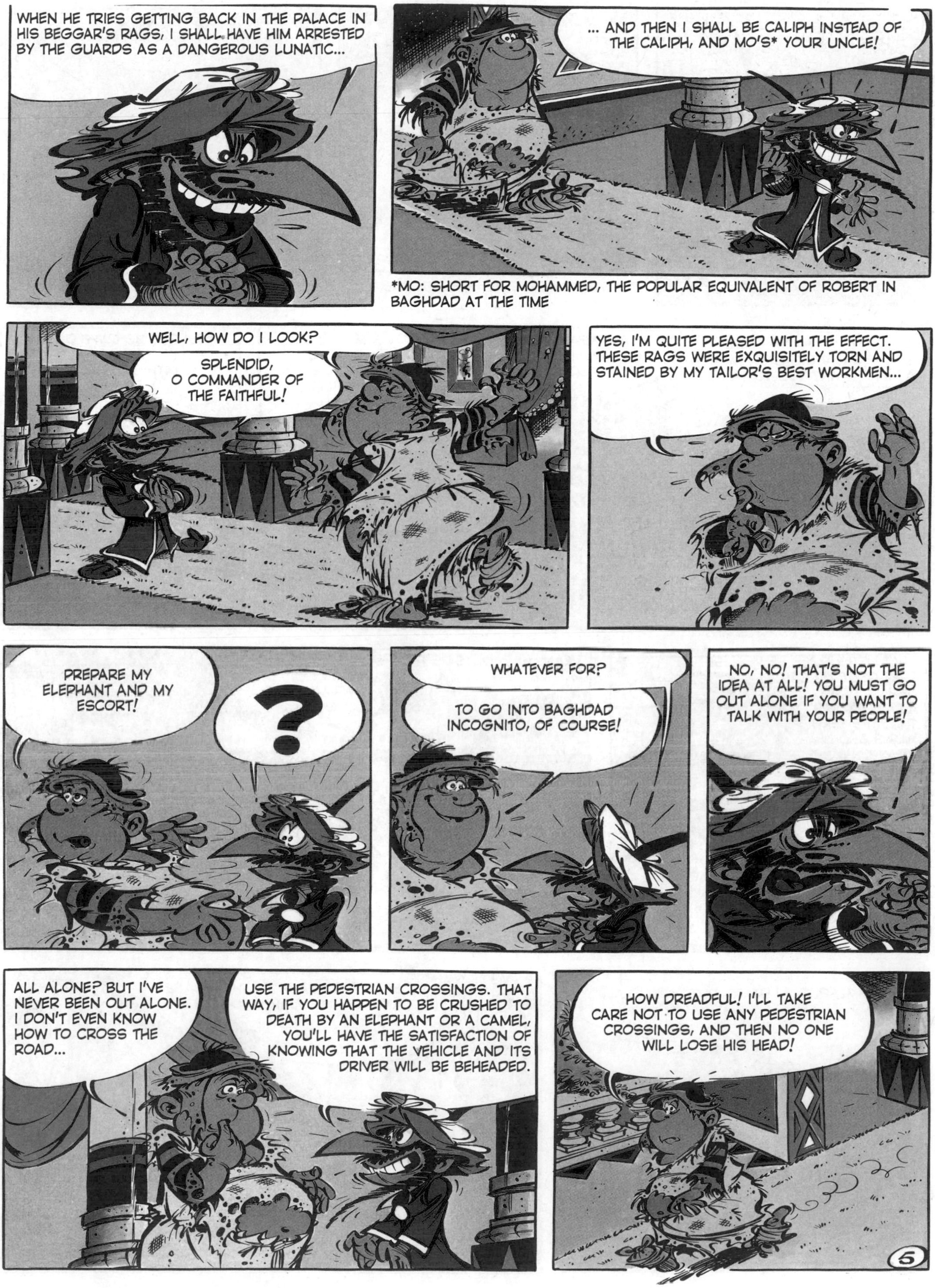
WHEN HE TRIES GETTING BACK IN THE PALACE IN HIS BEGGAR'S RAGS, I SHALL HAVE HIM ARRESTED BY THE GUARDS AS A DANGEROUS LUNATIC...
... AND THEN I SHALL BE CALIPH INSTEAD OF THE CALIPH, AND MO'S* YOUR UNCLE!
*MO: SHORT FOR MOHAMMED, THE POPULAR EQUIVALENT OF ROBERT IN BAGHDAD AT THE TIME
WELL, HOW DO I LOOK?
SPLENDID, O COMMANDER OF THE FAITHFUL!
YES, I'M QUITE PLEASED WITH THE EFFECT. THESE RAGS WERE EXQUISITELY TORN AND STAINED BY MY TAILOR'S BEST WORKMEN...
PREPARE MY ELEPHANT AND MY ESCORT!
?
WHATEVER FOR?
TO GO INTO BAGHDAD INCOGNITO, OF COURSE!
NO, NO! THAT'S NOT THE IDEA AT ALL! YOU MUST GO OUT ALONE IF YOU WANT TO TALK WITH YOUR PEOPLE!
ALL ALONE? BUT I'VE NEVER BEEN OUT ALONE. I DON'T EVEN KNOW HOW TO CROSS THE ROAD...
USE THE PEDESTRIAN CROSSINGS. THAT WAY, IF YOU HAPPEN TO BE CRUSHED TO DEATH BY AN ELEPHANT OR A CAMEL, YOU'LL HAVE THE SATISFACTION OF KNOWING THAT THE VEHICLE AND ITS DRIVER WILL BE BEHEADED.
HOW DREADFUL! I'LL TAKE CARE NOT TO USE ANY PEDESTRIAN CROSSINGS, AND THEN NO ONE WILL LOSE HIS HEAD!
5

HE'S GONE! HE'S GONE!

THE WICKED GRAND VIZIER IS SO HAPPY AT THE PROSPECT OF SUCCEEDING THE CALIPH THAT HE'S WALKING ON AIR.*

*IN OTHER WORDS, HE'S HEIRBORNE.

NOW TO FIND WA'AT ALAHF, MY FAITHFUL STRONG-ARM MAN...

AH, THERE YOU ARE! COME TO THE PALACE GATES, WA'AT ALAHF. I WANT YOU TO TAKE ORDERS.

YOU MEAN, BE A MULLAH, MASTER?

NO, NO! TAKE MY ORDERS, AND YOU WILL BECOME MY GRAND VIZIER BECAUSE I'M GOING TO BE CALIPH!

IS GRAND VIZIER A GOOD JOB?

YOU GET 26 DAYS OF PAID HOLIDAYS AND A BONUS MONTH'S PAY FOR THE NEW YEAR.

DADDY AND HIS HAREM WON'T BELIEVE HOW SUCCESSFUL I'VE BECOME!

AHA! LITTLE DOES HE REALISE THAT ONCE I'M CALIPH, I SHALL PASS A LAW SAYING THAT THE YEAR HAS 3,650 DAYS...

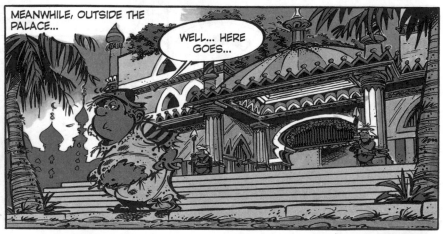

MEANWHILE, OUTSIDE THE PALACE...

WELL... HERE GOES...

HMM... BUT IF I START OUT, HOW SHALL I FIND MY WAY BACK?

I'D BETTER GO BACK TO THE PALACE AND ASK MY DEAR IZNOGOUD TO BE MY GUIDE...

6

26

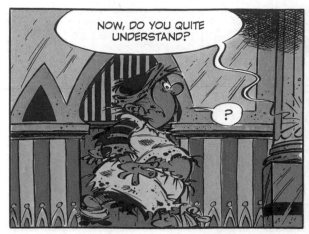

NOW, DO YOU QUITE UNDERSTAND?

?

IF A BEGGAR TURNS UP, YOU MUST GET THE GUARDS TO ARREST HIM AT ONCE. NO MATTER WHAT HE SAYS, HAVE HIM LOCKED UP IN THE DEEPEST DUNGEON IN THE PALACE!

I'LL BE OFF. MY DEAR IZNOGOUD IS BUSY: I MUSTN'T DISTURB HIM WHILE HE'S SO HARD AT WORK. I'LL FIND MY WAY SOMEHOW.

PLENTY OF SUBJECTS AROUND HERE... I'LL PICK ONE AT RANDOM AND ASK HIM MY QUESTION.

EXCUSE ME, MY GOOD MAN... WHAT DO YOU THINK OF ME?

?

I THINK YOU'RE A FAT MAN IN RAGS, AND I DON'T HAVE TIME TO WASTE TALKING TO FAT MEN IN RAGS!

OH, OF COURSE! HE DIDN'T RECOGNISE ME. HOW STUPID OF ME!

WELL, WHAT ABOUT THE CALIPH, MY GOOD MAN? WHAT DO YOU THINK OF THE CALIPH?

THE CALIPH? THE CALIPH IS AN AVARICIOUS TYRANT WHO IMPOSES PUNITIVE TAXES ON HIS LONG-SUFFERING PEOPLE!

THE CALIPH IS EMPTYING OUR POCKETS TO FEED HIS OWN BELLY!!
DOWN WITH HAROUN AL PLASSID!
!
WE HATE THE CALIPH!
I... I CAN ASSURE YOU THAT THAT WILL ALL BE CHANGED!
HAHAHA!
?!!
HOHOHO!
YOU POOR FOOL! HOW DO YOU THINK A MISERABLE BEGGAR LIKE YOU IS GOING TO PERSUADE THE ALL-POWERFUL CALIPH TO CHANGE THINGS?
I ABSOLUTELY MUST TELL MY DEAR IZNOGOUD TO REPEAL OUR LAWS. I'M SURE HE HAS NO IDEA THAT THE PEOPLE DON'T LIKE THEM.
LET'S SEE... I CAME THIS WAY...
AND THEN, I THINK IT WAS THAT WAY...
OR WAS IT THIS WAY...?
I'M LOST...
8

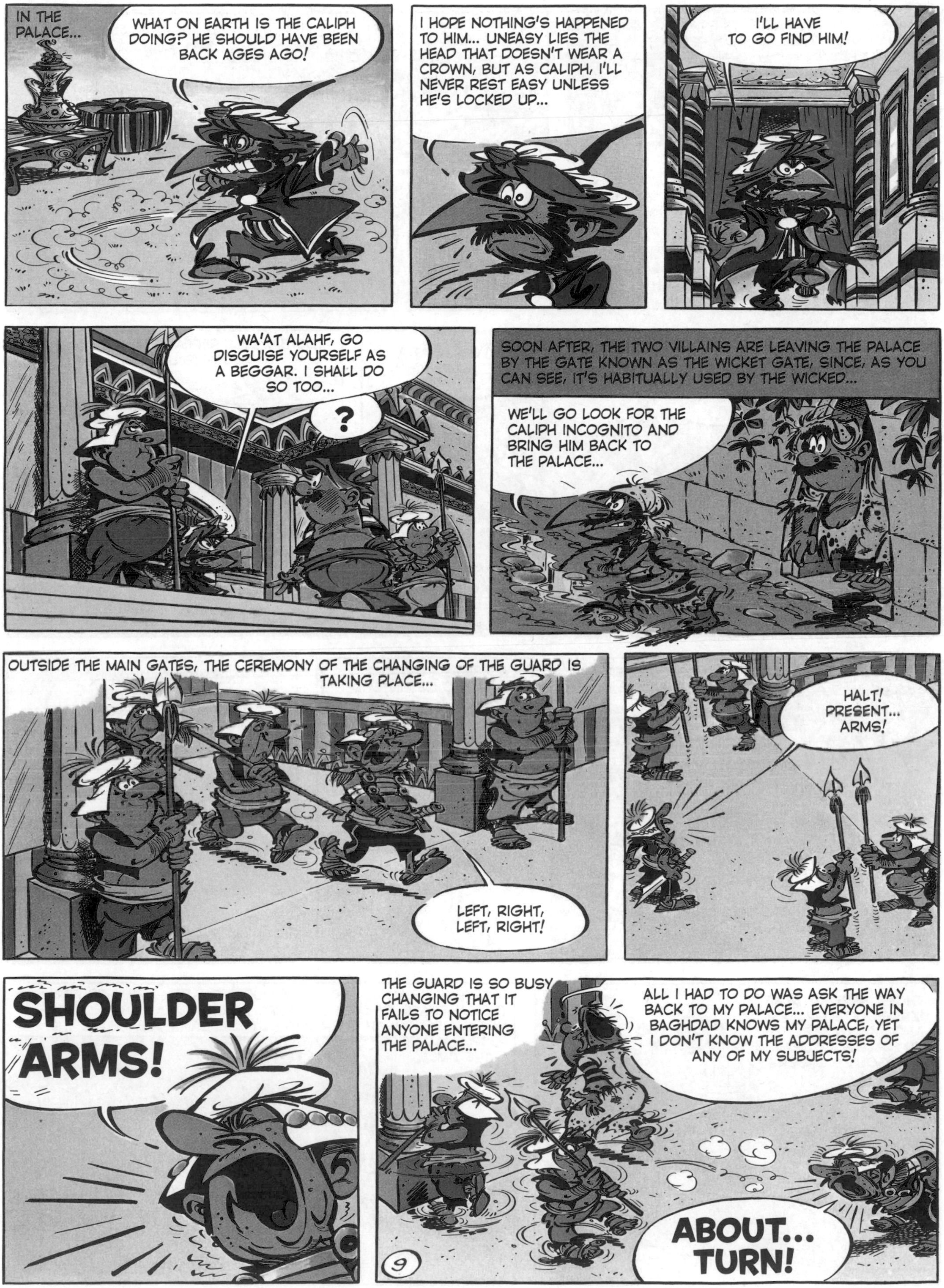
IN THE PALACE...
WHAT ON EARTH IS THE CALIPH DOING? HE SHOULD HAVE BEEN BACK AGES AGO!
I HOPE NOTHING'S HAPPENED TO HIM... UNEASY LIES THE HEAD THAT DOESN'T WEAR A CROWN, BUT AS CALIPH, I'LL NEVER REST EASY UNLESS HE'S LOCKED UP...
I'LL HAVE TO GO FIND HIM!
WA'AT ALAHF, GO DISGUISE YOURSELF AS A BEGGAR. I SHALL DO SO TOO...
?
SOON AFTER, THE TWO VILLAINS ARE LEAVING THE PALACE BY THE GATE KNOWN AS THE WICKET GATE, SINCE, AS YOU CAN SEE, IT'S HABITUALLY USED BY THE WICKED...
WE'LL GO LOOK FOR THE CALIPH INCOGNITO AND BRING HIM BACK TO THE PALACE...
OUTSIDE THE MAIN GATES, THE CEREMONY OF THE CHANGING OF THE GUARD IS TAKING PLACE...
LEFT, RIGHT, LEFT, RIGHT!
HALT! PRESENT... ARMS!
SHOULDER ARMS!
THE GUARD IS SO BUSY CHANGING THAT IT FAILS TO NOTICE ANYONE ENTERING THE PALACE...
ALL I HAD TO DO WAS ASK THE WAY BACK TO MY PALACE... EVERYONE IN BAGHDAD KNOWS MY PALACE, YET I DON'T KNOW THE ADDRESSES OF ANY OF MY SUBJECTS!
ABOUT... TURN!
9

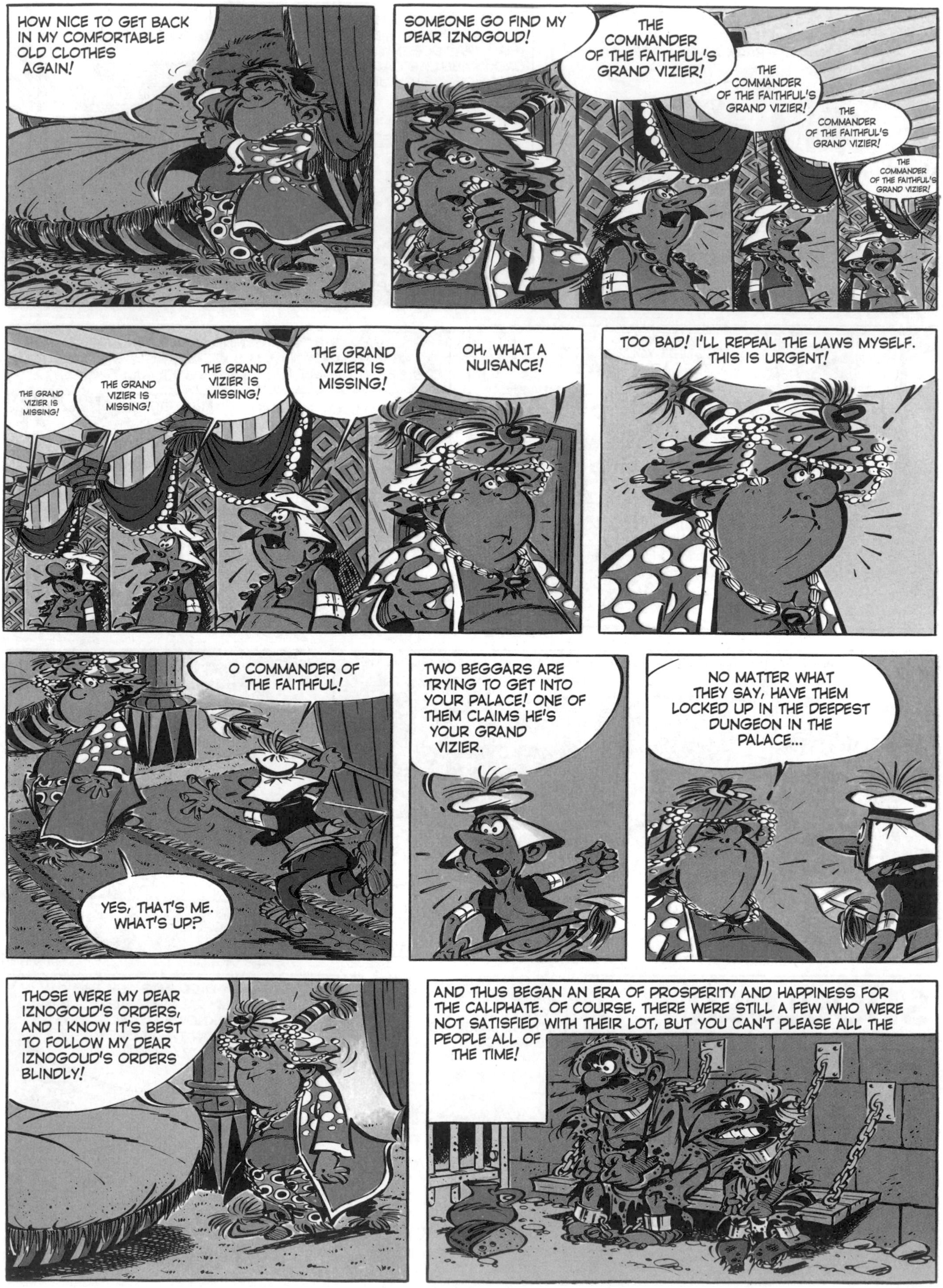

HOW NICE TO GET BACK IN MY COMFORTABLE OLD CLOTHES AGAIN!
SOMEONE GO FIND MY DEAR IZNOGOUD!
THE COMMANDER OF THE FAITHFUL'S GRAND VIZIER!
THE COMMANDER OF THE FAITHFUL'S GRAND VIZIER!
THE COMMANDER OF THE FAITHFUL'S GRAND VIZIER!
THE COMMANDER OF THE FAITHFUL'S GRAND VIZIER!
THE GRAND VIZIER IS MISSING!
THE GRAND VIZIER IS MISSING!
THE GRAND VIZIER IS MISSING!
THE GRAND VIZIER IS MISSING!
OH, WHAT A NUISANCE!
TOO BAD! I'LL REPEAL THE LAWS MYSELF. THIS IS URGENT!
O COMMANDER OF THE FAITHFUL!
YES, THAT'S ME. WHAT'S UP?
TWO BEGGARS ARE TRYING TO GET INTO YOUR PALACE! ONE OF THEM CLAIMS HE'S YOUR GRAND VIZIER.
NO MATTER WHAT THEY SAY, HAVE THEM LOCKED UP IN THE DEEPEST DUNGEON IN THE PALACE...
THOSE WERE MY DEAR IZNOGOUD'S ORDERS, AND I KNOW IT'S BEST TO FOLLOW MY DEAR IZNOGOUD'S ORDERS BLINDLY!
AND THUS BEGAN AN ERA OF PROSPERITY AND HAPPINESS FOR THE CALIPHATE. OF COURSE, THERE WERE STILL A FEW WHO WERE NOT SATISFIED WITH THEIR LOT, BUT YOU CAN'T PLEASE ALL THE PEOPLE ALL OF THE TIME!

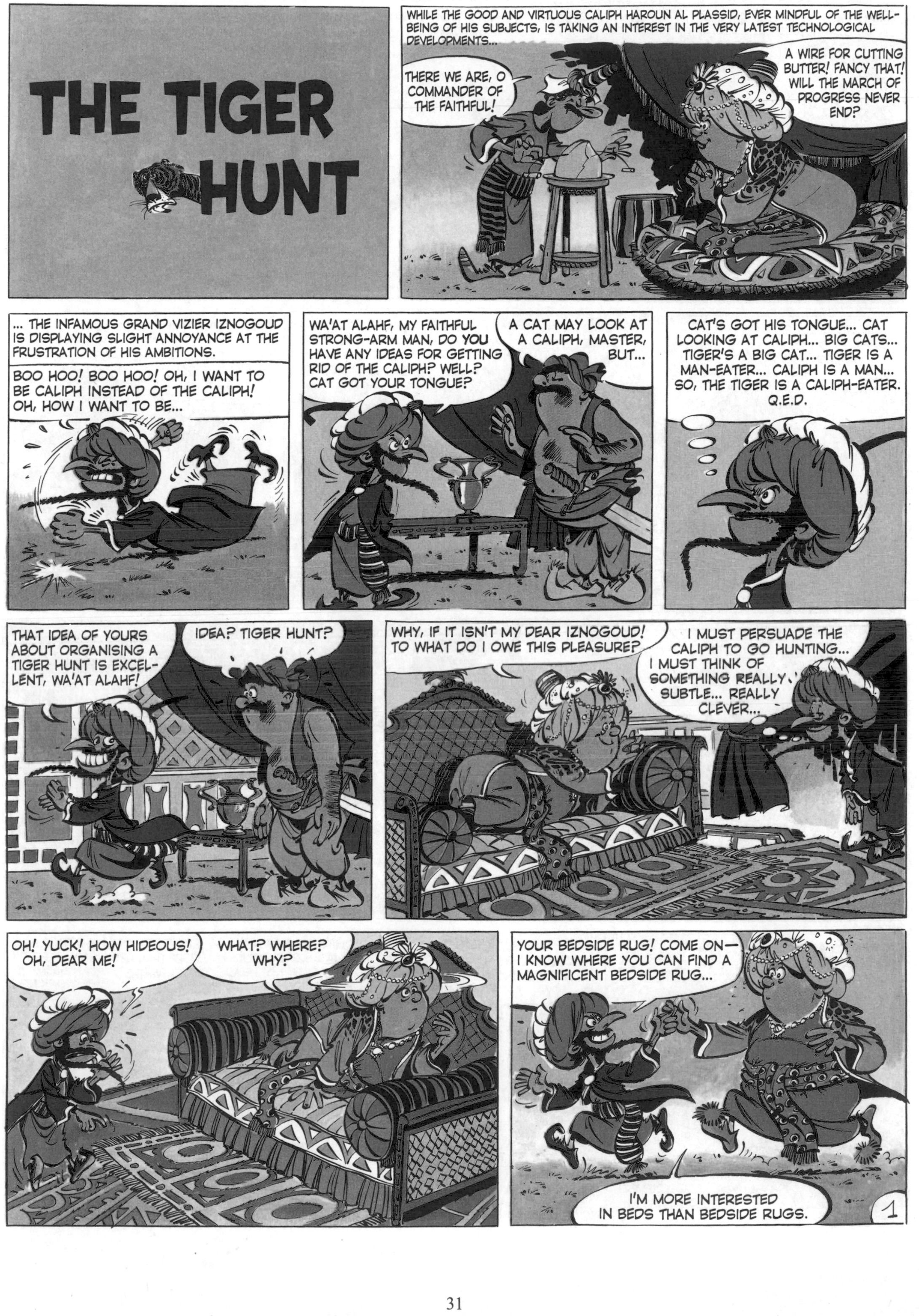
THE TIGER HUNT
WHILE THE GOOD AND VIRTUOUS CALIPH HAROUN AL PLASSID, EVER MINDFUL OF THE WELL-BEING OF HIS SUBJECTS, IS TAKING AN INTEREST IN THE VERY LATEST TECHNOLOGICAL DEVELOPMENTS...
THERE WE ARE, O COMMANDER OF THE FAITHFUL!
A WIRE FOR CUTTING BUTTER! FANCY THAT! WILL THE MARCH OF PROGRESS NEVER END?
... THE INFAMOUS GRAND VIZIER IZNOGOUD IS DISPLAYING SLIGHT ANNOYANCE AT THE FRUSTRATION OF HIS AMBITIONS.
BOO HOO! BOO HOO! OH, I WANT TO BE CALIPH INSTEAD OF THE CALIPH! OH, HOW I WANT TO BE...
WA'AT ALAHF, MY FAITHFUL STRONG-ARM MAN, DO YOU HAVE ANY IDEAS FOR GETTING RID OF THE CALIPH? WELL? CAT GOT YOUR TONGUE?
A CAT MAY LOOK AT A CALIPH, MASTER, BUT...
CAT'S GOT HIS TONGUE... CAT LOOKING AT CALIPH... BIG CATS... TIGER'S A BIG CAT... TIGER IS A MAN-EATER... CALIPH IS A MAN... SO, THE TIGER IS A CALIPH-EATER. Q.E.D.
THAT IDEA OF YOURS ABOUT ORGANISING A TIGER HUNT IS EXCEL-LENT, WA'AT ALAHF!
IDEA? TIGER HUNT?
WHY, IF IT ISN'T MY DEAR IZNOGOUD! TO WHAT DO I OWE THIS PLEASURE?
I MUST PERSUADE THE CALIPH TO GO HUNTING... I MUST THINK OF SOMETHING REALLY SUBTLE... REALLY CLEVER...
OH! YUCK! HOW HIDEOUS! OH, DEAR ME!
WHAT? WHERE? WHY?
YOUR BEDSIDE RUG! COME ON— I KNOW WHERE YOU CAN FIND A MAGNIFICENT BEDSIDE RUG...
I'M MORE INTERESTED IN BEDS THAN BEDSIDE RUGS.
1

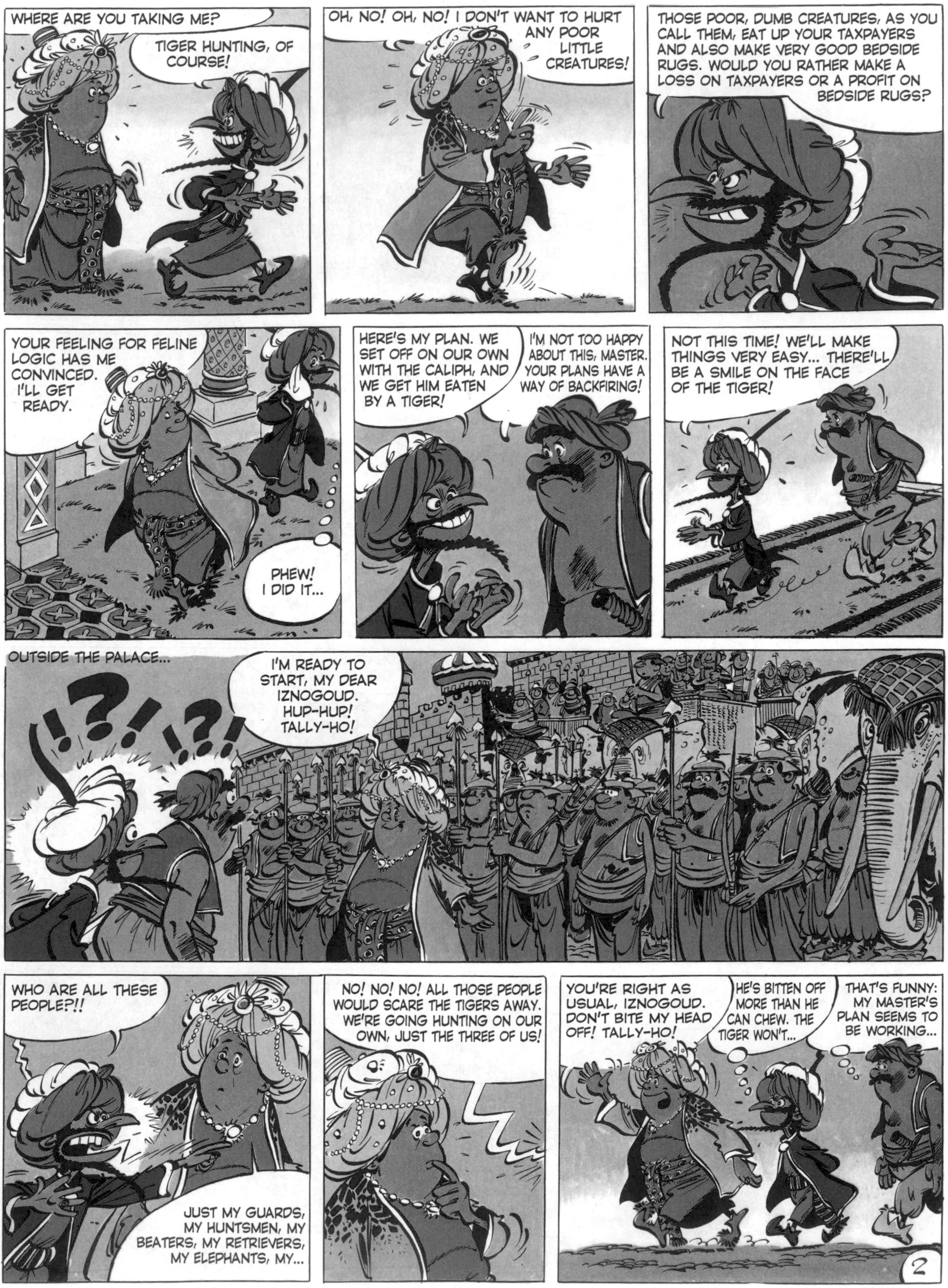
WHERE ARE YOU TAKING ME?
TIGER HUNTING, OF COURSE!
OH, NO! OH, NO! I DON'T WANT TO HURT ANY POOR LITTLE CREATURES!
THOSE POOR, DUMB CREATURES, AS YOU CALL THEM, EAT UP YOUR TAXPAYERS AND ALSO MAKE VERY GOOD BEDSIDE RUGS. WOULD YOU RATHER MAKE A LOSS ON TAXPAYERS OR A PROFIT ON BEDSIDE RUGS?
YOUR FEELING FOR FELINE LOGIC HAS ME CONVINCED. I'LL GET READY.
PHEW! I DID IT...
HERE'S MY PLAN. WE SET OFF ON OUR OWN WITH THE CALIPH, AND WE GET HIM EATEN BY A TIGER!
I'M NOT TOO HAPPY ABOUT THIS, MASTER. YOUR PLANS HAVE A WAY OF BACKFIRING!
NOT THIS TIME! WE'LL MAKE THINGS VERY EASY... THERE'LL BE A SMILE ON THE FACE OF THE TIGER!
OUTSIDE THE PALACE...
I'M READY TO START, MY DEAR IZNOGOUD. HUP-HUP! TALLY-HO!
!?!!?!
WHO ARE ALL THESE PEOPLE?!!
JUST MY GUARDS, MY HUNTSMEN, MY BEATERS, MY RETRIEVERS, MY ELEPHANTS, MY...
NO! NO! NO! ALL THOSE PEOPLE WOULD SCARE THE TIGERS AWAY. WE'RE GOING HUNTING ON OUR OWN, JUST THE THREE OF US!
YOU'RE RIGHT AS USUAL, IZNOGOUD. DON'T BITE MY HEAD OFF! TALLY-HO!
HE'S BITTEN OFF MORE THAN HE CAN CHEW. THE TIGER WON'T...
THAT'S FUNNY: MY MASTER'S PLAN SEEMS TO BE WORKING...
2

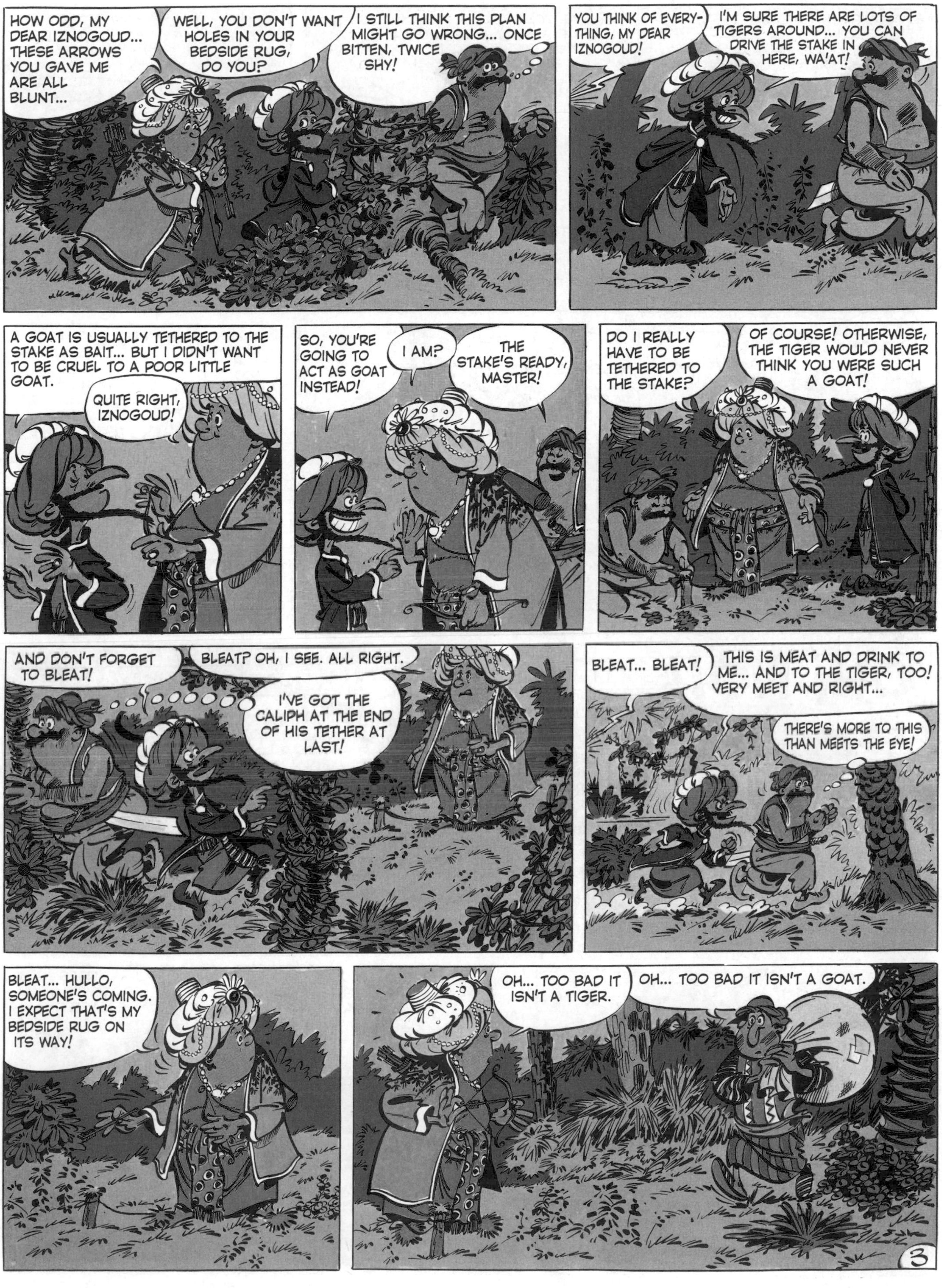

HOW ODD, MY DEAR IZNOGOUD... THESE ARROWS YOU GAVE ME ARE ALL BLUNT...
WELL, YOU DON'T WANT HOLES IN YOUR BEDSIDE RUG, DO YOU?
I STILL THINK THIS PLAN MIGHT GO WRONG... ONCE BITTEN, TWICE SHY!
YOU THINK OF EVERY-THING, MY DEAR IZNOGOUD!
I'M SURE THERE ARE LOTS OF TIGERS AROUND... YOU CAN DRIVE THE STAKE IN HERE, WA'AT!
A GOAT IS USUALLY TETHERED TO THE STAKE AS BAIT... BUT I DIDN'T WANT TO BE CRUEL TO A POOR LITTLE GOAT.
QUITE RIGHT, IZNOGOUD!
SO, YOU'RE GOING TO ACT AS GOAT INSTEAD!
I AM?
THE STAKE'S READY, MASTER!
DO I REALLY HAVE TO BE TETHERED TO THE STAKE?
OF COURSE! OTHERWISE, THE TIGER WOULD NEVER THINK YOU WERE SUCH A GOAT!
AND DON'T FORGET TO BLEAT!
BLEAT? OH, I SEE. ALL RIGHT.
I'VE GOT THE CALIPH AT THE END OF HIS TETHER AT LAST!
BLEAT... BLEAT!
THIS IS MEAT AND DRINK TO ME... AND TO THE TIGER, TOO! VERY MEET AND RIGHT...
THERE'S MORE TO THIS THAN MEETS THE EYE!
BLEAT... HULLO, SOMEONE'S COMING. I EXPECT THAT'S MY BEDSIDE RUG ON ITS WAY!
OH... TOO BAD IT ISN'T A TIGER.
OH... TOO BAD IT ISN'T A GOAT.
3

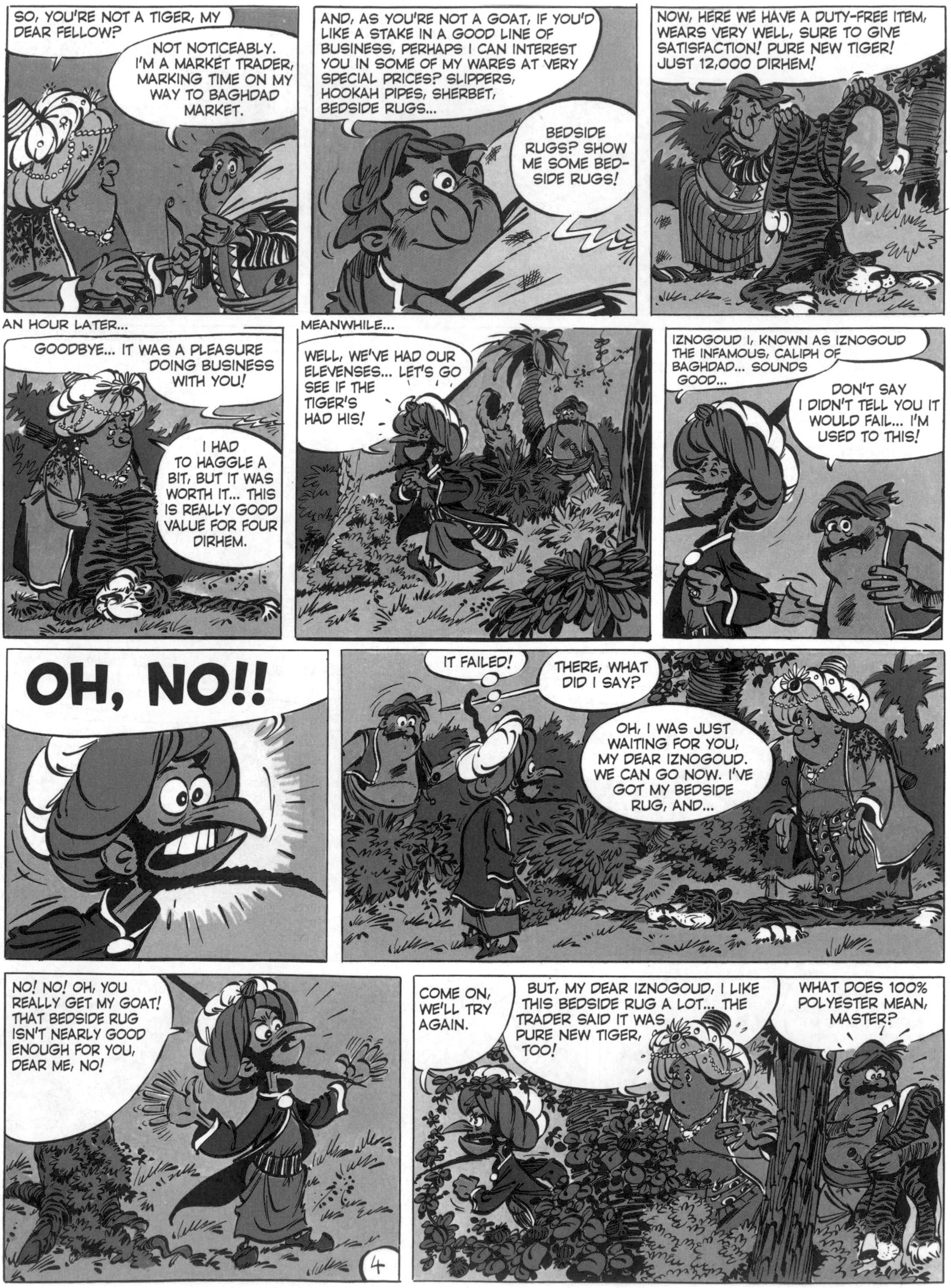

SO, YOU'RE NOT A TIGER, MY DEAR FELLOW?
NOT NOTICEABLY. I'M A MARKET TRADER, MARKING TIME ON MY WAY TO BAGHDAD MARKET.
AND, AS YOU'RE NOT A GOAT, IF YOU'D LIKE A STAKE IN A GOOD LINE OF BUSINESS, PERHAPS I CAN INTEREST YOU IN SOME OF MY WARES AT VERY SPECIAL PRICES? SLIPPERS, HOOKAH PIPES, SHERBET, BEDSIDE RUGS...
BEDSIDE RUGS? SHOW ME SOME BEDSIDE RUGS!
NOW, HERE WE HAVE A DUTY-FREE ITEM, WEARS VERY WELL, SURE TO GIVE SATISFACTION! PURE NEW TIGER! JUST 12,000 DIRHEM!
AN HOUR LATER...
GOODBYE... IT WAS A PLEASURE DOING BUSINESS WITH YOU!
I HAD TO HAGGLE A BIT, BUT IT WAS WORTH IT... THIS IS REALLY GOOD VALUE FOR FOUR DIRHEM.
MEANWHILE...
WELL, WE'VE HAD OUR ELEVENSES... LET'S GO SEE IF THE TIGER'S HAD HIS!
IZNOGOUD I, KNOWN AS IZNOGOUD THE INFAMOUS, CALIPH OF BAGHDAD... SOUNDS GOOD...
DON'T SAY I DIDN'T TELL YOU IT WOULD FAIL... I'M USED TO THIS!
OH, NO!!
IT FAILED!
THERE, WHAT DID I SAY?
OH, I WAS JUST WAITING FOR YOU, MY DEAR IZNOGOUD. WE CAN GO NOW. I'VE GOT MY BEDSIDE RUG, AND...
NO! NO! OH, YOU REALLY GET MY GOAT! THAT BEDSIDE RUG ISN'T NEARLY GOOD ENOUGH FOR YOU, DEAR ME, NO!
4
COME ON, WE'LL TRY AGAIN.
BUT, MY DEAR IZNOGOUD, I LIKE THIS BEDSIDE RUG A LOT... THE TRADER SAID IT WAS PURE NEW TIGER, TOO!
WHAT DOES 100% POLYESTER MEAN, MASTER?

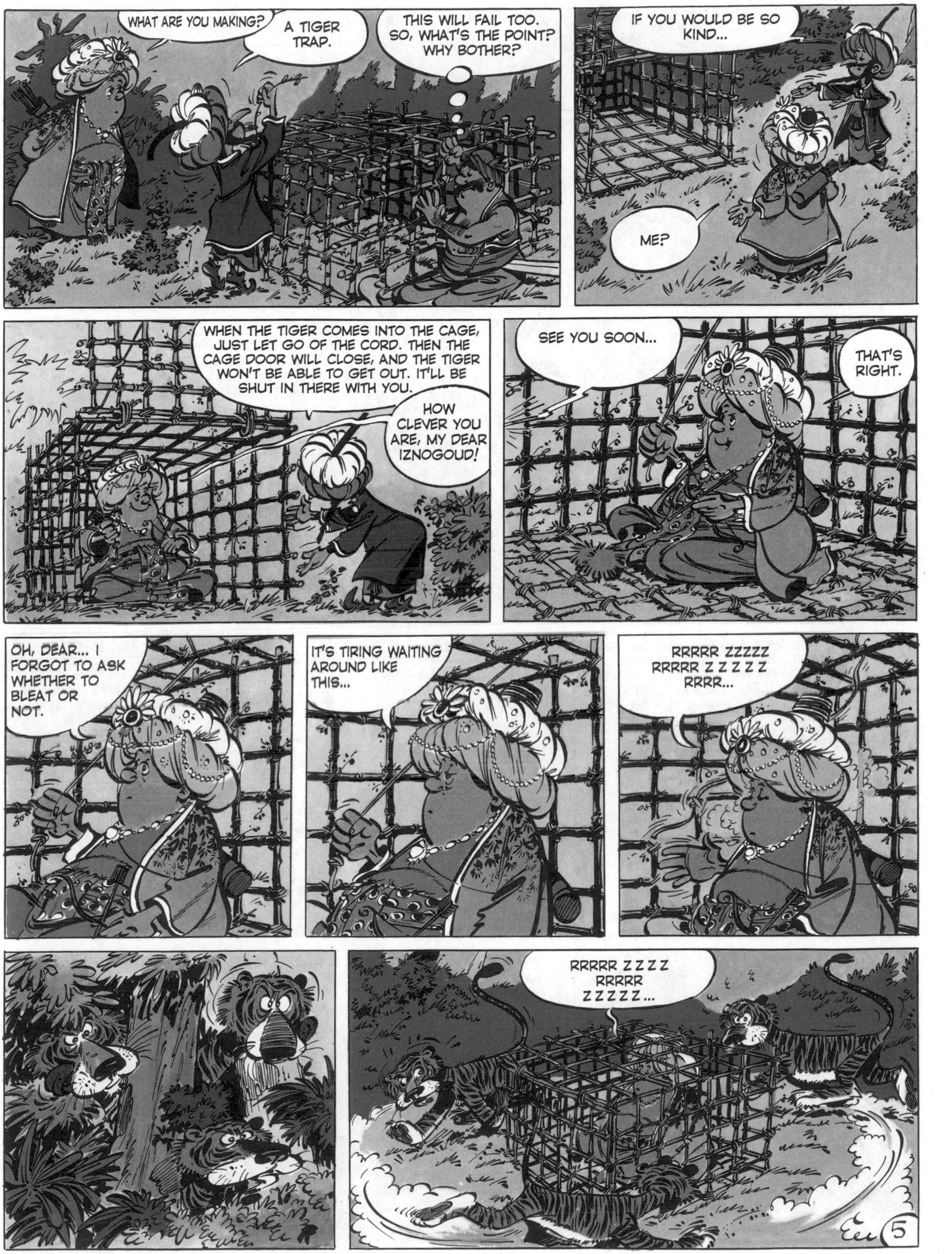
WHAT ARE YOU MAKING?
A TIGER TRAP.
THIS WILL FAIL TOO. SO, WHAT'S THE POINT? WHY BOTHER?
IF YOU WOULD BE SO KIND...
ME?
WHEN THE TIGER COMES INTO THE CAGE, JUST LET GO OF THE CORD. THEN THE CAGE DOOR WILL CLOSE, AND THE TIGER WON'T BE ABLE TO GET OUT. IT'LL BE SHUT IN THERE WITH YOU.
HOW CLEVER YOU ARE, MY DEAR IZNOGOUD!
SEE YOU SOON...
THAT'S RIGHT.
OH, DEAR... I FORGOT TO ASK WHETHER TO BLEAT OR NOT.
IT'S TIRING WAITING AROUND LIKE THIS...
RRRRR ZZZZZ RRRRR Z Z Z Z Z RRRR...
RRRRR Z Z Z Z RRRRR Z Z Z Z Z...
5

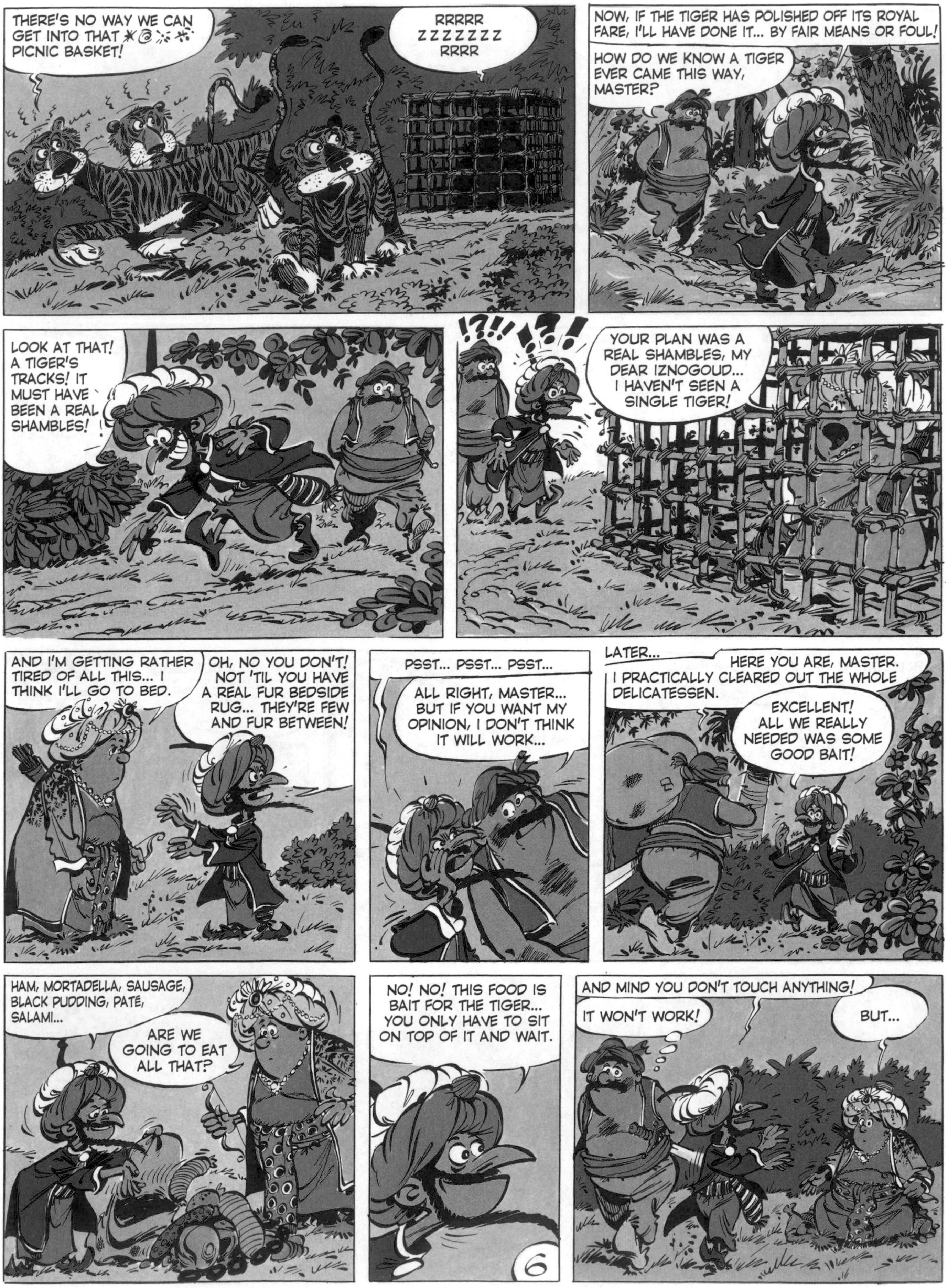
THERE'S NO WAY WE CAN GET INTO THAT PICNIC BASKET!
RRRRR ZZZZZZZ RRRR
NOW, IF THE TIGER HAS POLISHED OFF ITS ROYAL FARE, I'LL HAVE DONE IT... BY FAIR MEANS OR FOUL!
HOW DO WE KNOW A TIGER EVER CAME THIS WAY, MASTER?
LOOK AT THAT! A TIGER'S TRACKS! IT MUST HAVE BEEN A REAL SHAMBLES!
!?!!! !?!
YOUR PLAN WAS A REAL SHAMBLES, MY DEAR IZNOGOUD... I HAVEN'T SEEN A SINGLE TIGER!
AND I'M GETTING RATHER TIRED OF ALL THIS... I THINK I'LL GO TO BED.
OH, NO YOU DON'T! NOT 'TIL YOU HAVE A REAL FUR BEDSIDE RUG... THEY'RE FEW AND FUR BETWEEN!
PSST... PSST... PSST...
ALL RIGHT, MASTER... BUT IF YOU WANT MY OPINION, I DON'T THINK IT WILL WORK...
LATER...
HERE YOU ARE, MASTER. I PRACTICALLY CLEARED OUT THE WHOLE DELICATESSEN.
EXCELLENT! ALL WE REALLY NEEDED WAS SOME GOOD BAIT!
HAM, MORTADELLA, SAUSAGE, BLACK PUDDING, PATÉ, SALAMI...
ARE WE GOING TO EAT ALL THAT?
NO! NO! THIS FOOD IS BAIT FOR THE TIGER... YOU ONLY HAVE TO SIT ON TOP OF IT AND WAIT.
6
AND MIND YOU DON'T TOUCH ANYTHING!
IT WON'T WORK!
BUT...

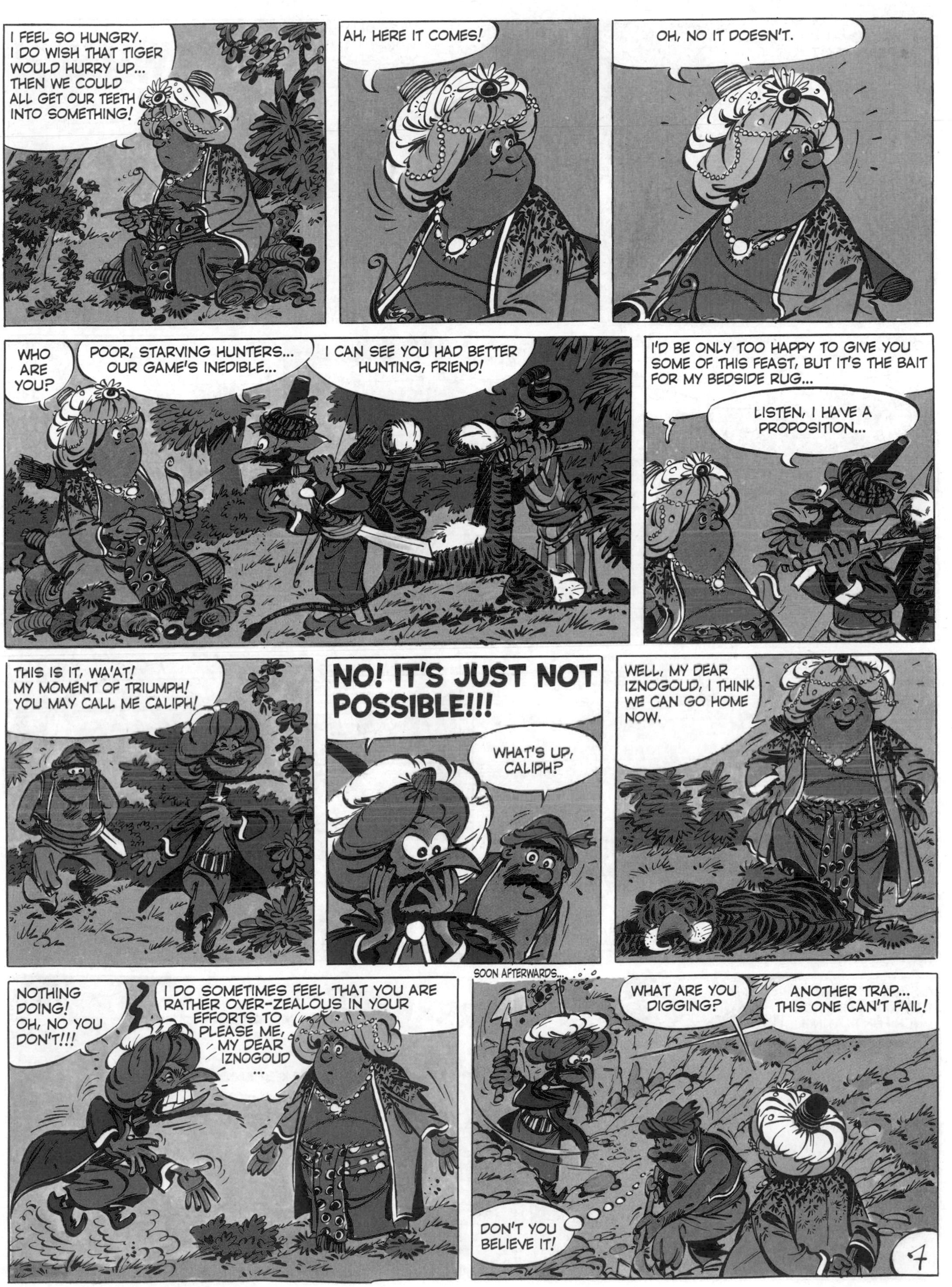
I FEEL SO HUNGRY. I DO WISH THAT TIGER WOULD HURRY UP... THEN WE COULD ALL GET OUR TEETH INTO SOMETHING!
AH, HERE IT COMES!
OH, NO IT DOESN'T.
WHO ARE YOU?
POOR, STARVING HUNTERS... OUR GAME'S INEDIBLE...
I CAN SEE YOU HAD BETTER HUNTING, FRIEND!
I'D BE ONLY TOO HAPPY TO GIVE YOU SOME OF THIS FEAST, BUT IT'S THE BAIT FOR MY BEDSIDE RUG...
LISTEN, I HAVE A PROPOSITION...
THIS IS IT, WA'AT! MY MOMENT OF TRIUMPH! YOU MAY CALL ME CALIPH!
NO! IT'S JUST NOT POSSIBLE!!!
WHAT'S UP, CALIPH?
WELL, MY DEAR IZNOGOUD, I THINK WE CAN GO HOME NOW.
NOTHING DOING! OH, NO YOU DON'T!!!
I DO SOMETIMES FEEL THAT YOU ARE RATHER OVER-ZEALOUS IN YOUR EFFORTS TO PLEASE ME, MY DEAR IZNOGOUD ...
SOON AFTERWARDS...
WHAT ARE YOU DIGGING?
ANOTHER TRAP... THIS ONE CAN'T FAIL!
DON'T YOU BELIEVE IT!
4

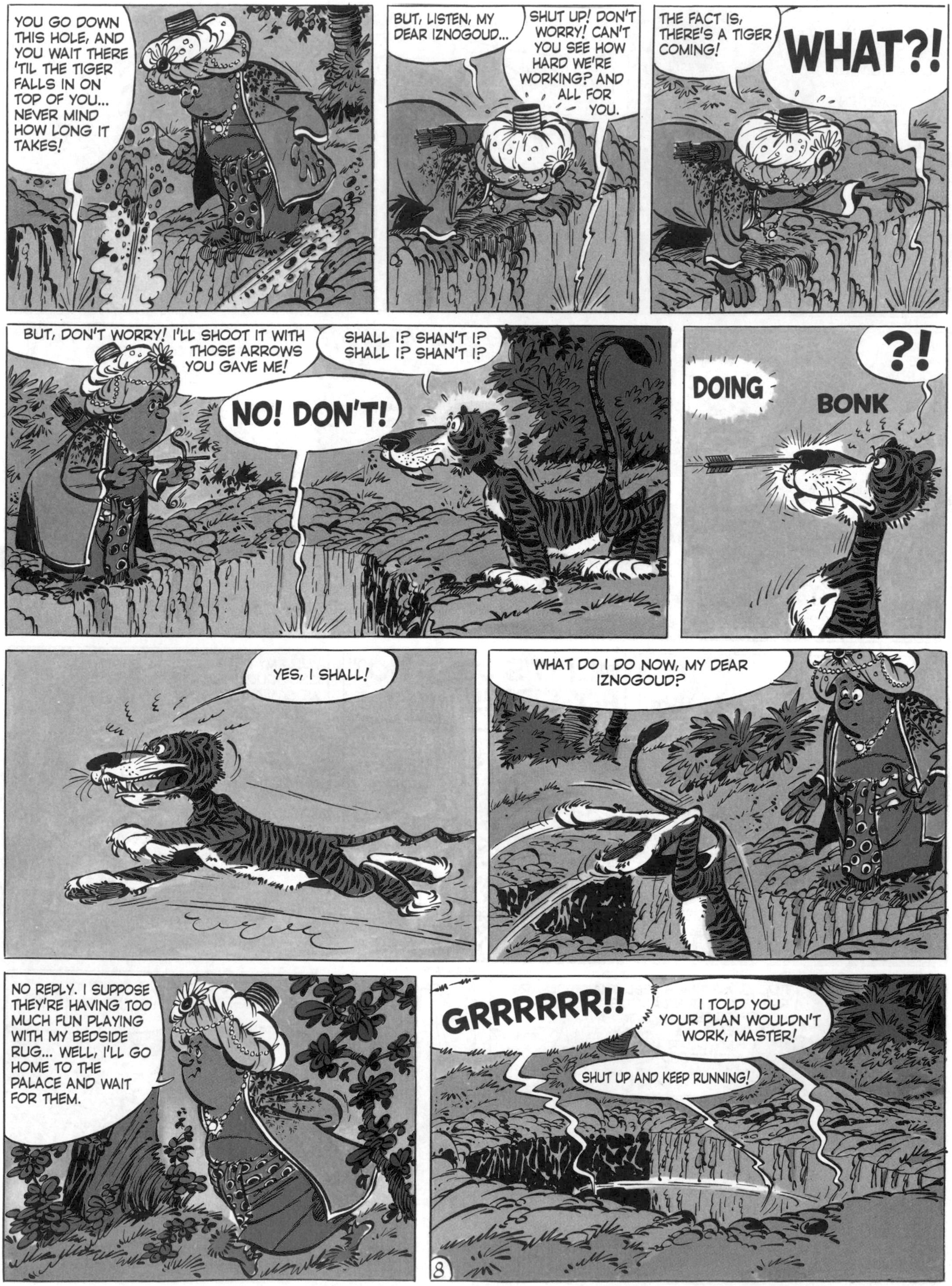

YOU GO DOWN THIS HOLE, AND YOU WAIT THERE 'TIL THE TIGER FALLS IN ON TOP OF YOU... NEVER MIND HOW LONG IT TAKES!
BUT, LISTEN, MY DEAR IZNOGOUD...
SHUT UP! DON'T WORRY! CAN'T YOU SEE HOW HARD WE'RE WORKING? AND ALL FOR YOU.
THE FACT IS, THERE'S A TIGER COMING!
WHAT?!
BUT, DON'T WORRY! I'LL SHOOT IT WITH THOSE ARROWS YOU GAVE ME!
SHALL I? SHAN'T I? SHALL I? SHAN'T I?
NO! DON'T!
DOING
BONK
?!
YES, I SHALL!
WHAT DO I DO NOW, MY DEAR IZNOGOUD?
NO REPLY. I SUPPOSE THEY'RE HAVING TOO MUCH FUN PLAYING WITH MY BEDSIDE RUG... WELL, I'LL GO HOME TO THE PALACE AND WAIT FOR THEM.
GRRRRRR!!
I TOLD YOU YOUR PLAN WOULDN'T WORK, MASTER!
SHUT UP AND KEEP RUNNING!
8

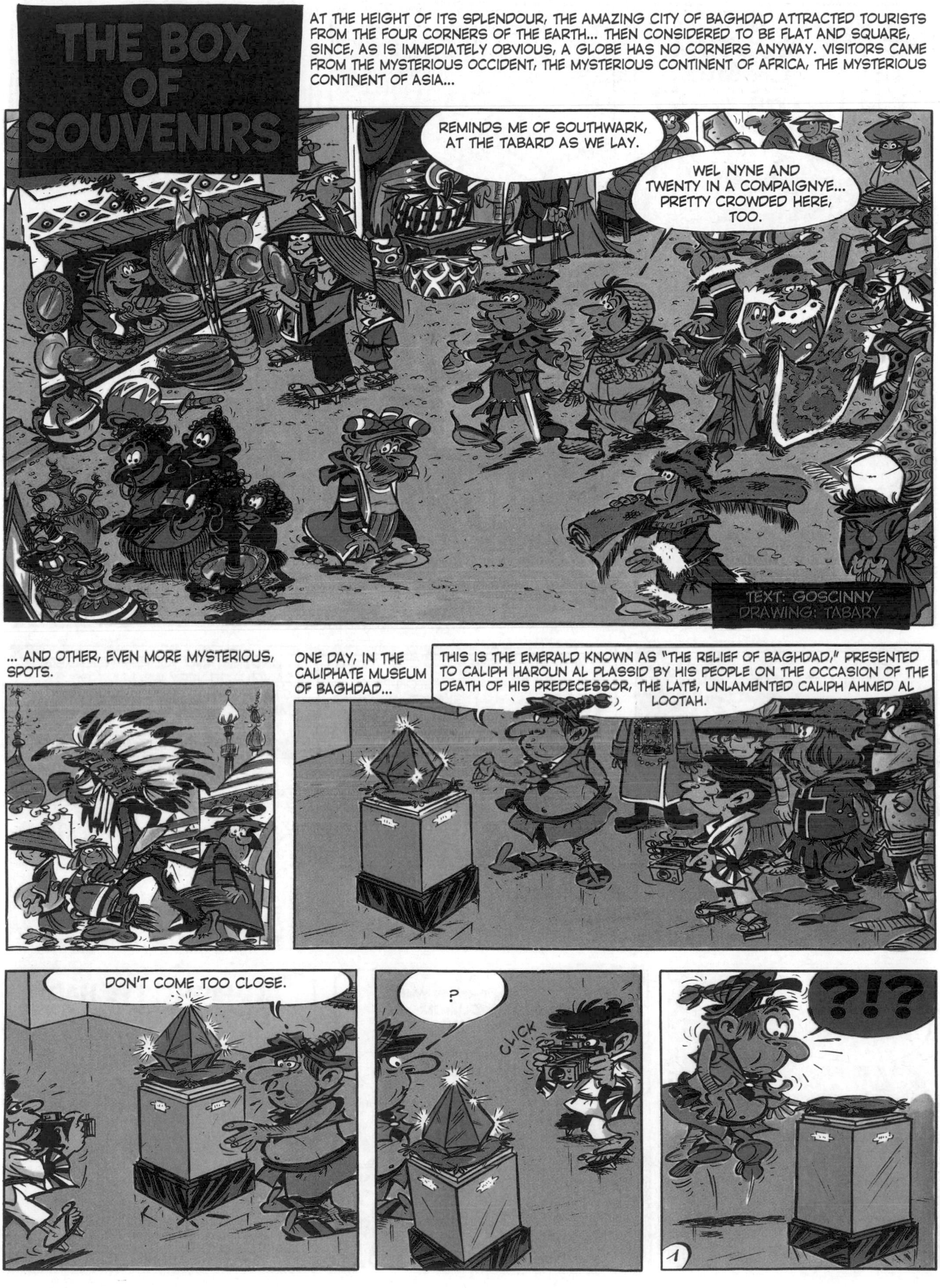
THE BOX OF SOUVENIRS
AT THE HEIGHT OF ITS SPLENDOUR, THE AMAZING CITY OF BAGHDAD ATTRACTED TOURISTS FROM THE FOUR CORNERS OF THE EARTH... THEN CONSIDERED TO BE FLAT AND SQUARE, SINCE, AS IS IMMEDIATELY OBVIOUS, A GLOBE HAS NO CORNERS ANYWAY. VISITORS CAME FROM THE MYSTERIOUS OCCIDENT, THE MYSTERIOUS CONTINENT OF AFRICA, THE MYSTERIOUS CONTINENT OF ASIA...
REMINDS ME OF SOUTHWARK, AT THE TABARD AS WE LAY.
WEL NYNE AND TWENTY IN A COMPAIGNYE... PRETTY CROWDED HERE, TOO.
TEXT: GOSCINNY
DRAWING: TABARY
... AND OTHER, EVEN MORE MYSTERIOUS, SPOTS.
ONE DAY, IN THE CALIPHATE MUSEUM OF BAGHDAD...
THIS IS THE EMERALD KNOWN AS "THE RELIEF OF BAGHDAD," PRESENTED TO CALIPH HAROUN AL PLASSID BY HIS PEOPLE ON THE OCCASION OF THE DEATH OF HIS PREDECESSOR, THE LATE, UNLAMENTED CALIPH AHMED AL LOOTAH.
DON'T COME TOO CLOSE.
?
CLICK
?!?
1

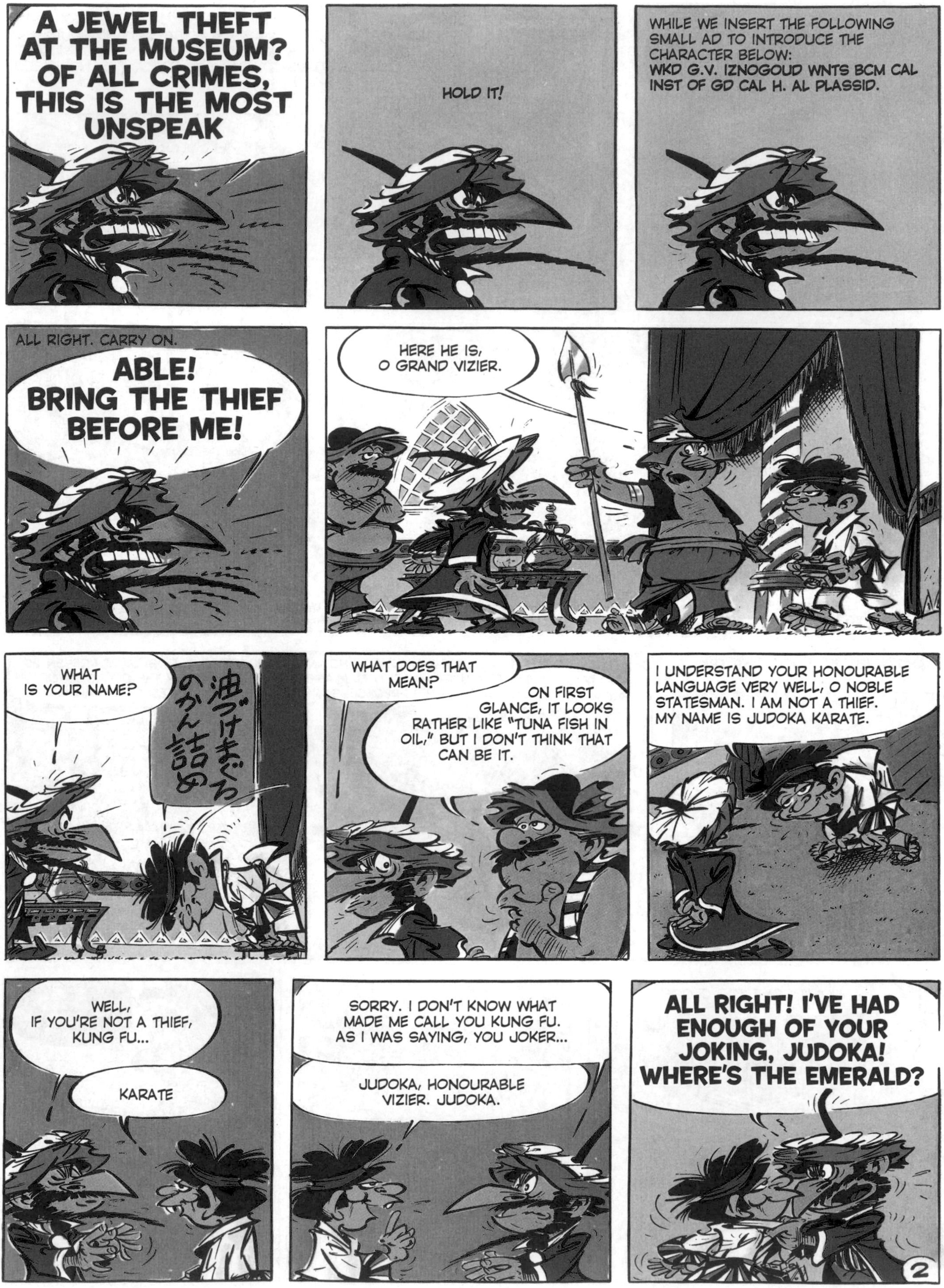
A JEWEL THEFT AT THE MUSEUM? OF ALL CRIMES, THIS IS THE MOST UNSPEAK
HOLD IT!
WHILE WE INSERT THE FOLLOWING SMALL AD TO INTRODUCE THE CHARACTER BELOW:
WKD G.V. IZNOGOUD WNTS BCM CAL INST OF GD CAL H. AL PLASSID.
ALL RIGHT. CARRY ON.
ABLE! BRING THE THIEF BEFORE ME!
HERE HE IS, O GRAND VIZIER.
WHAT IS YOUR NAME?
油づけまぐろのかん詰め
WHAT DOES THAT MEAN?
ON FIRST GLANCE, IT LOOKS RATHER LIKE "TUNA FISH IN OIL," BUT I DON'T THINK THAT CAN BE IT.
I UNDERSTAND YOUR HONOURABLE LANGUAGE VERY WELL, O NOBLE STATESMAN. I AM NOT A THIEF. MY NAME IS JUDOKA KARATE.
WELL, IF YOU'RE NOT A THIEF, KUNG FU...
KARATE
SORRY. I DON'T KNOW WHAT MADE ME CALL YOU KUNG FU. AS I WAS SAYING, YOU JOKER...
JUDOKA, HONOURABLE VIZIER. JUDOKA.
ALL RIGHT! I'VE HAD ENOUGH OF YOUR JOKING, JUDOKA! WHERE'S THE EMERALD?
2

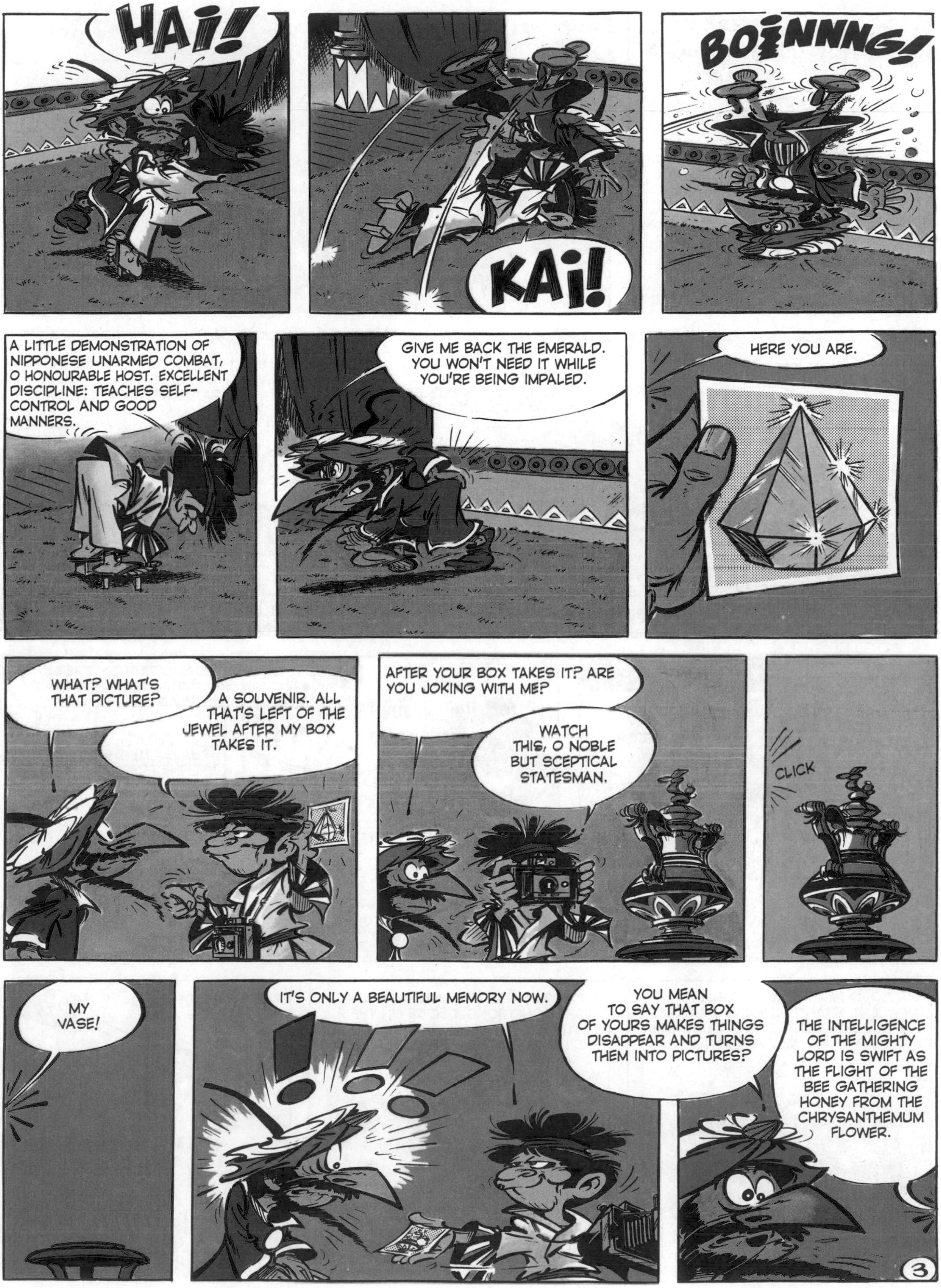
HAI!
KAI!
BOINNNG!
A LITTLE DEMONSTRATION OF NIPPONESE UNARMED COMBAT, O HONOURABLE HOST. EXCELLENT DISCIPLINE: TEACHES SELF-CONTROL AND GOOD MANNERS.
GIVE ME BACK THE EMERALD. YOU WON'T NEED IT WHILE YOU'RE BEING IMPALED.
HERE YOU ARE.
WHAT? WHAT'S THAT PICTURE?
A SOUVENIR. ALL THAT'S LEFT OF THE JEWEL AFTER MY BOX TAKES IT.
AFTER YOUR BOX TAKES IT? ARE YOU JOKING WITH ME?
WATCH THIS, O NOBLE BUT SCEPTICAL STATESMAN.
CLICK
MY VASE!
IT'S ONLY A BEAUTIFUL MEMORY NOW.
YOU MEAN TO SAY THAT BOX OF YOURS MAKES THINGS DISAPPEAR AND TURNS THEM INTO PICTURES?
THE INTELLIGENCE OF THE MIGHTY LORD IS SWIFT AS THE FLIGHT OF THE BEE GATHERING HONEY FROM THE CHRYSANTHEMUM FLOWER.
3

IF WE WERE NIPPY ENOUGH WITH THAT BOX FROM WHOSIT...

NIPPON, NOT WHOSIT...

NIPPON NOT WHOSIT? IS THERE A PUN IN THAT?

HE SHOULD KNOW: HE'S THE PUNDIT.

NOW, LISTEN, UJOKA KAWASAKI, DOES THAT BOX OF YOURS WORK WITH LIVING CREATURES?

JUDOKA KARATE. YES, EXCEPT WITH LITTLE BIRDIES, WHICH TEND TO COME BACK OUT OF THE BOX AGAIN.

SEE MY SOUVENIRS: PICTURES OF MY REVERED MOTHER-IN-LAW, MY HIGHLY RESPECTED TAX INSPECTOR, A DEAR FRIEND WHO LENT ME MONEY... I HAVE 12 ALBUMS OF PICTURES BACK HOME.

HOW MUCH IS YOUR BOX?

MEMORIES ARE PRICELESS... BUT I'M POOR, IT'S TRUE.

MY WIFE IS KNOWN AS MADAME BUTTERFLY BECAUSE WE KEEP FLITTING WHEN THE RENT IS DUE. WE KARATES ARE NOT VERY GOOD BUSINESSMEN, SO...

TWELVE DIRHEM.

TO MAKE A LONG STORY SHORT, AFTER A MOST COURTEOUS DISCUSSION...

221,000; 222,000; 223,005.72 DIRHEM... YES, THAT'S IT!

I'LL TRY IT OUT RIGHT NOW!

NO, MASTER! DON'T!

CLICK

YOU'RE STILL THERE! I'VE BEEN HAD! I DIDN'T READ THE FINE PRINT!

PHEW! SAVED BY THE FINE PRINT!

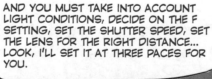

NO, NO, O PERSPICACIOUS BUT IMPATIENT GRAND VIZIER IN A HURRY. THE SUBJECT MUST STAND QUITE STILL OR THE PICTURE WILL NOT COME OUT.

OH.

AND YOU MUST TAKE INTO ACCOUNT LIGHT CONDITIONS, DECIDE ON THE F SETTING, SET THE SHUTTER SPEED, SET THE LENS FOR THE RIGHT DISTANCE... LOOK, I'LL SET IT AT THREE PACES FOR YOU.

THERE. SEE THAT WALL THREE PACES AWAY?

?

4

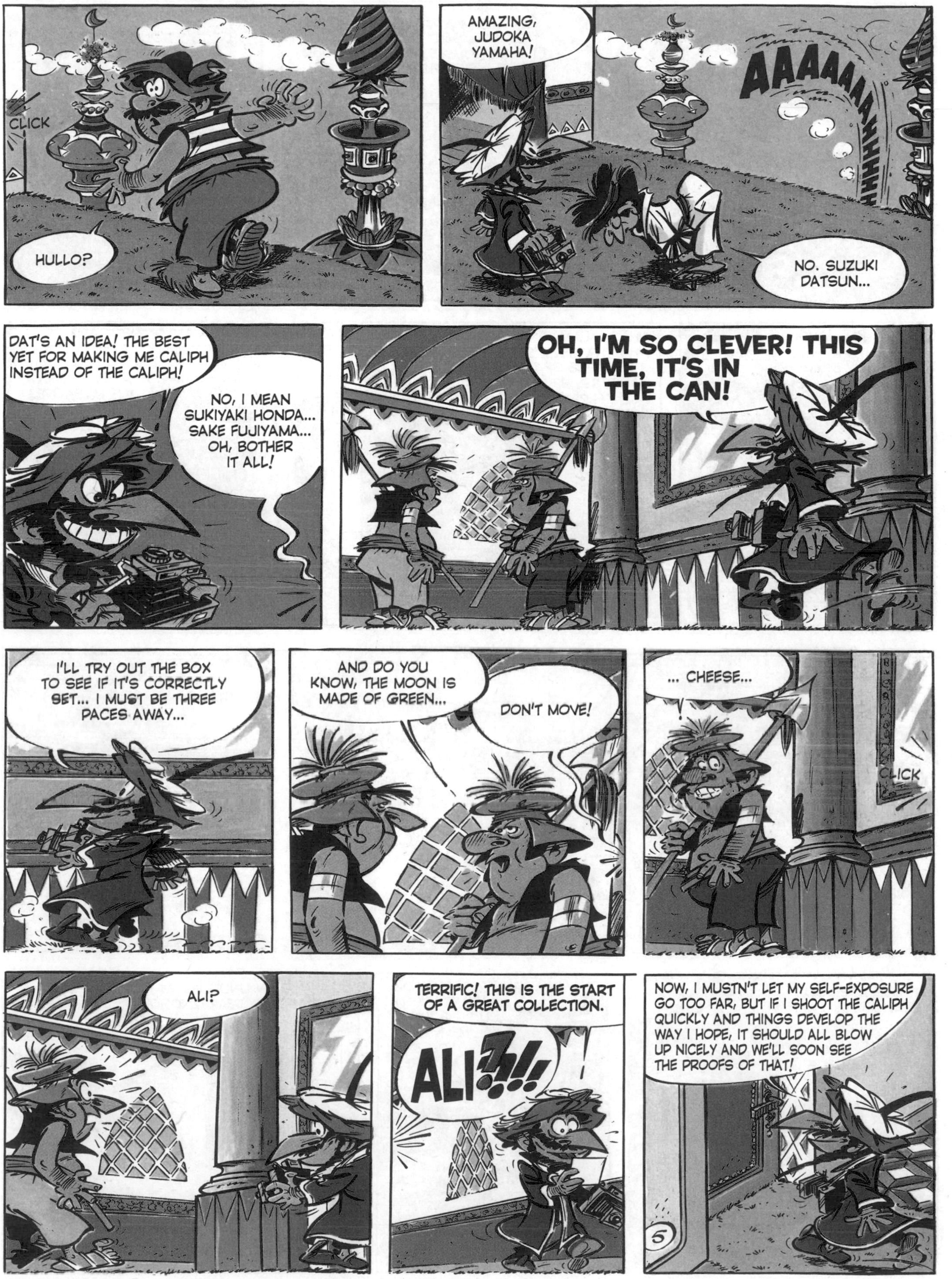
CLICK
HULLO?
AMAZING, JUDOKA YAMAHA!
AAAAAAAHHHHHH
NO. SUZUKI DATSUN...
DAT'S AN IDEA! THE BEST YET FOR MAKING ME CALIPH INSTEAD OF THE CALIPH!
NO, I MEAN SUKIYAKI HONDA... SAKE FUJIYAMA... OH, BOTHER IT ALL!
OH, I'M SO CLEVER! THIS TIME, IT'S IN THE CAN!
I'LL TRY OUT THE BOX TO SEE IF IT'S CORRECTLY SET... I MUST BE THREE PACES AWAY...
AND DO YOU KNOW, THE MOON IS MADE OF GREEN...
DON'T MOVE!
... CHEESE...
CLICK
ALI?
TERRIFIC! THIS IS THE START OF A GREAT COLLECTION.
ALI?!!
NOW, I MUSTN'T LET MY SELF-EXPOSURE GO TOO FAR, BUT IF I SHOOT THE CALIPH QUICKLY AND THINGS DEVELOP THE WAY I HOPE, IT SHOULD ALL BLOW UP NICELY AND WE'LL SOON SEE THE PROOFS OF THAT!
5

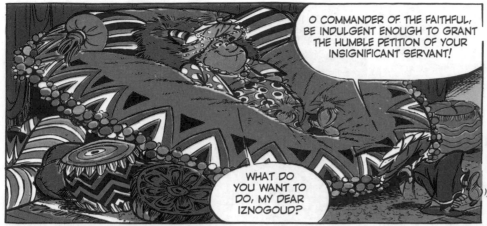

O COMMANDER OF THE FAITHFUL, BE INDULGENT ENOUGH TO GRANT THE HUMBLE PETITION OF YOUR INSIGNIFICANT SERVANT!

WHAT DO YOU WANT TO DO, MY DEAR IZNOGOUD?

EXECUTE YOUR PORTRAIT.

I DIDN'T KNOW YOU HAVE ANY ARTISTIC TALENT, MY DEAR IZNOGOUD.

LOOK AT THIS.

WHAT AN AMAZING LIKENESS... I KNOW WHO THAT IS. IT'S ALI, WHO USED TO BE ONE OF THE PRISON WARDENS. HE HAD TO BE TRANSFERRED TO THE PALACE; THE PRISONERS DIDN'T CARE FOR HIM.

THEY BEGGED FOR ANYONE BUT ALI. DO YOU KNOW HIM WELL?

THE ANSWER'S IN THE NEGATIVE. NOW, STAND THERE.

I'LL MEASURE IT OUT. I DON'T WANT TO GET YOUR PICTURE WRONG. OKAY, LET'S GO!

LET'S GO!

ONE... TWO...

THR...?

WHERE ARE YOU GOING?

NO IDEA. YOU SAID: LET'S GO!

ONLY IN A MANNER OF SPEAKING. I MEANT MYSELF. LET'S GO! THAT MEANS ME. YOU STAY HERE.

?

YOU HAVE AN UNUSUAL WAY OF PAINTING PORTRAITS, MY DEAR IZNOGOUD.

SSH. ONE... TWO...

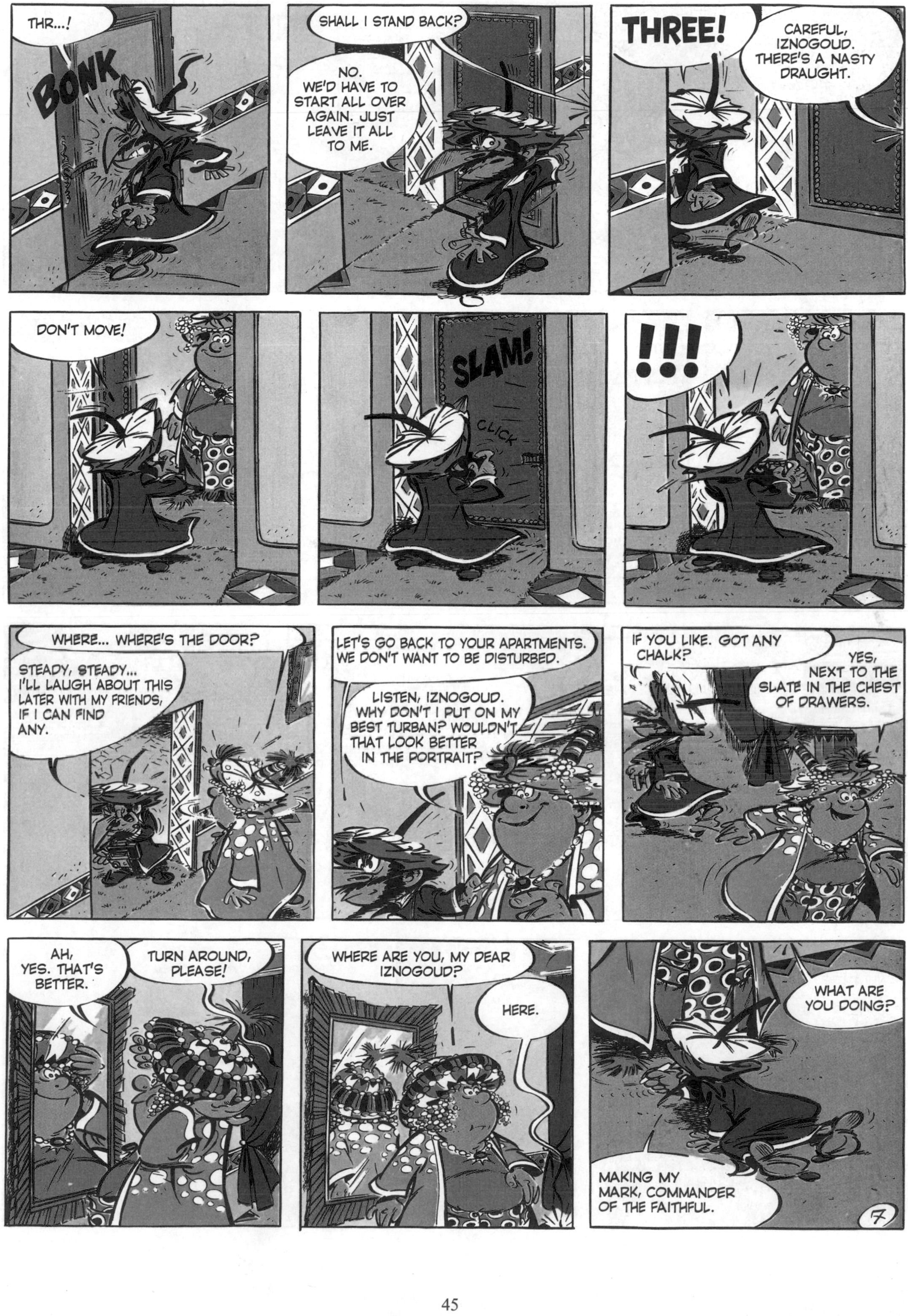
THR...!
BONK
SHALL I STAND BACK?
NO. WE'D HAVE TO START ALL OVER AGAIN. JUST LEAVE IT ALL TO ME.
THREE!
CAREFUL, IZNOGOUD. THERE'S A NASTY DRAUGHT.
DON'T MOVE!
SLAM!
CLICK
!!!
WHERE... WHERE'S THE DOOR?
STEADY, STEADY... I'LL LAUGH ABOUT THIS LATER WITH MY FRIENDS, IF I CAN FIND ANY.
LET'S GO BACK TO YOUR APARTMENTS. WE DON'T WANT TO BE DISTURBED.
LISTEN, IZNOGOUD. WHY DON'T I PUT ON MY BEST TURBAN? WOULDN'T THAT LOOK BETTER IN THE PORTRAIT?
IF YOU LIKE. GOT ANY CHALK?
YES, NEXT TO THE SLATE IN THE CHEST OF DRAWERS.
AH, YES. THAT'S BETTER.
TURN AROUND, PLEASE!
WHERE ARE YOU, MY DEAR IZNOGOUD?
HERE.
WHAT ARE YOU DOING?
MAKING MY MARK, COMMANDER OF THE FAITHFUL.
7

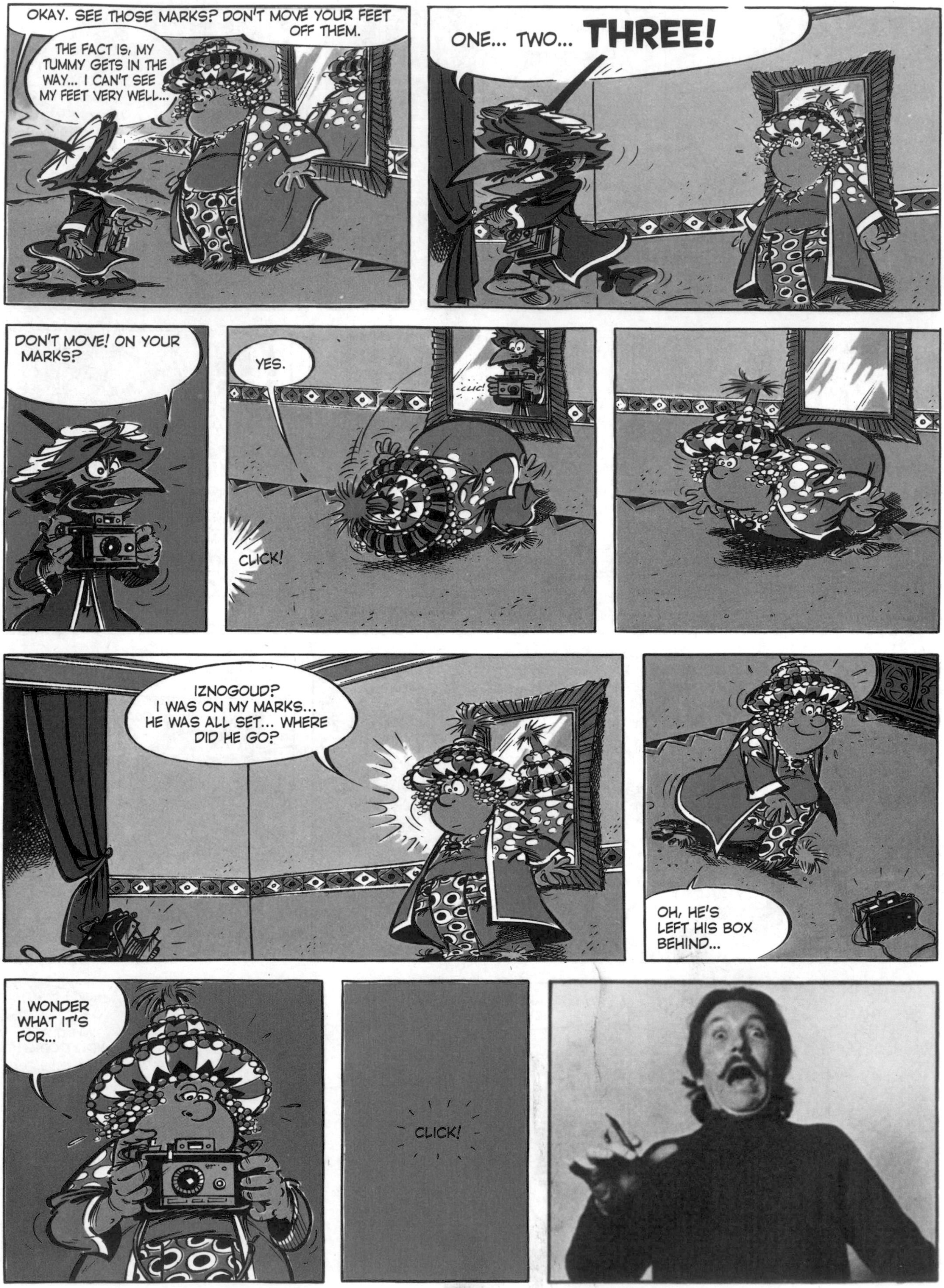
OKAY. SEE THOSE MARKS? DON'T MOVE YOUR FEET OFF THEM.
THE FACT IS, MY TUMMY GETS IN THE WAY... I CAN'T SEE MY FEET VERY WELL...
ONE... TWO... THREE!
DON'T MOVE! ON YOUR MARKS?
YES.
CLICK!
IZNOGOUD? I WAS ON MY MARKS... HE WAS ALL SET... WHERE DID HE GO?
OH, HE'S LEFT HIS BOX BEHIND...
I WONDER WHAT IT'S FOR...
CLICK!

IZNOGOUD

GOSCINNY - TABARY
THE WICKED WILES OF
IZNOGOUD

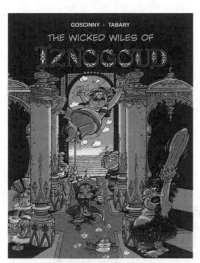

1 - THE WICKED WILES OF IZNOGOUD

GOSCINNY - TABARY
IZNOGOUD
THE CALIPH'S VACATION

2 - THE CALIPH'S VACATION

GOSCINNY - TABARY
IZNOGOUD
AND THE DAY OF MISRULE

3 - IZNOGOUD AND THE DAY OF MISRULE

GOSCINNY - TABARY
IZNOGOUD
AND THE MAGIC COMPUTER

4 - IZNOGOUD AND THE MAGIC COMPUTER

GOSCINNY - TABARY
A CARROT FOR
IZNOGOUD

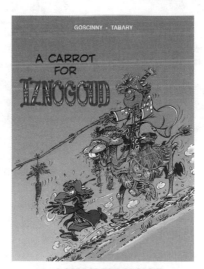

5 - A CARROT FOR IZNOGOUD

GOSCINNY - TABARY
IZNOGOUD
AND THE MAGIC CARPET

6 - IZNOGOUD AND THE MAGIC CARPET

IZNOGOUD

COMING SOON

GOSCINNY - TABARY
IZNOGOUD
THE INFAMOUS

7 - IZNOGOUD THE INFAMOUS

GOSCINNY - TABARY
IZNOGOUD
ROCKETS TO
STARDOM

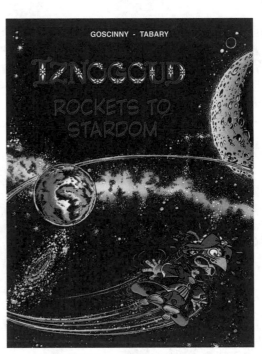

8 - IZNOGOUD ROCKETS TO STARDOM